ANTHONY COLLINS

A DISCOURSE

CONCERNING

Ridicule and Irony

IN WRITING

(1729)

Introduction by
EDWARD A. BLOOM AND LILLIAN D. BLOOM

WILDSIDE PRESS

INTRODUCTION

Between 1710 and 1729 Anthony Collins was lampooned,
satirized, and gravely denounced from pulpit and press as England's most insidious defiler of church and state. Yet within a
year of his death he became the model of a proper country gentleman,

> . . . he had an opulent Fortune, descended to him from
> his Ancestors, which he left behind him unimpair'd:
> He lived on his own Estate in the Country, where his
> Tenants paid him moderate Rents, which he never en-
> hanced on their making any Improvements; he always
> oblig'd his Family to a constant attendance on Publick
> Worship; as he was himself a Man of the strictest
> Morality, for he never suffer'd any Body about him who
> was deficient in that Point; he exercised a universal
> Charity to all Sorts of People, without any Regard
> either to Sect or Party; being in the Commission of
> the Peace, he administred Justice with such Impar-
> tiality and Incorruptness, that the most distant Part
> of the County flock'd to his Decisions; but the chief
> Use he made of his Authority was in accommodating
> Differences; . . .[1]

In a comparison which likens him to Sir Roger de Coverley, there
is less truth than fiction. What they did share was a love of the
countryside and a "universal Charity" towards its inhabitants.
For the most part, however, we can approximate Collins's per-
sonality by reversing many of Sir Roger's traits. Often at war
with his world, as the spectatorial character was not, he managed
to maintain an intellectual rapport with it and even with those
who sought his humiliation. He never—as an instance—disguised
his philosophical distrust of Samuel Clarke; yet during any debate
he planned "most certainly [to] outdo him in civility and good
manners."[2] This decorum in no way compromised his pursuit of
what he considered objective truth or his denunciation of all

"methods" or impositions of spiritual tyranny. Thus, during the virulent, uneven battle which followed upon the publication of the *Discourse of Free-Thinking*, he ignored his own wounds in order to applaud a critic's

> *suspicions that there is a sophism* in what he calls my *hypothesis.* That is a temper that ought to go thro' all our Inquirys, and especially before we have an opportunity of examining things to the bottom. It is safest at all times, and we are least likely to be mistaken, if we constantly suspect our selves to be under mistakes. . . . I have no system to defend or that I would seem to defend, and am unconcerned for the consequence that may be drawn from my opinion; and therefore stand clear of all difficultys wch others either by their opinion or caution are involved in.[3]

This is the statement of a man whose intellectual and religious commitment makes him see that his own fallibility is symptomatic of a human tendency to error. For himself, hence, he tries to avoid all manner of hard-voiced enthusiasm. Paradoxically, however, Collins searched with a zealot's avidity for any controversy which would either assert his faith or test his disbelief. When once he found his engagement, he revelled in it, whether as the aggressor or the harassed defendant. For example, in the "Preface" to the *Scheme of Literal Prophecy Considered* he boastfully enumerated all the works—some twenty-nine— which had repudiated his earlier *Discourse on the Grounds and Reasons of the Christian Religion*. And in malicious fact he held up the publication of the *Scheme* for almost a year that he might add a "Postscript to the Preface" in which he identified six more pieces hostile to the *Grounds and Reasons*.[4]

By May of 1727 and with no visible sign of fatigue he took on a new contender; this time it was John Rogers, canon in ordinary to the Prince of Wales. At the height of their debate, in late summer, Collins made practical enquiries about methods to prolong and intensify its give-and-take. Thus, in a note to his friend Pierre Des Maizeaux, he said: "But I would be particularly informed of the success and sale of the Letter to Dr Rogers;

because, if it could be, I would add to a new edition thereof two or three as sheets; which also might be sold separately to those who have already that Letter." For all his militant polemic, he asked only that his "Adversaries" observe with him a single rule of fair play; namely, that they refrain from name-calling and petty sniping. "Personal matters," he asserted, "tho they may some times afford useful remarks, are little regarded by Readers, who are very seldom mistaken in judging that the most impertinent subject a man can talk of is himself," particularly when he inveighs against another.[5]

If Collins had been made to look back over the years 1676–1729, he probably would have summarized the last twenty with a paraphrase of the Popean line, "This long controversy, my life." For several years and in such works as *Priestcraft in Perfection* (1710) and *A Discourse of Free-Thinking* (1713), he was a flailing polemicist against the entire Anglican hierarchy. Not until 1724 did he become a polished debater, when he initiated a controversy which for the next five years made a "very great noise" and which ended only with his death. The loudest shot in the persistent barrage was sounded by the *Grounds and Reasons,* and its last fusillade by the *Discourse concerning Ridicule and Irony in Writing.*[6]

During those five years Collins concentrated upon a single opponent in each work and made it a rhetorical practice to change his "Adversary" in successive essays. He created in this way a composite victim whose strength was lessened by deindividualization; in this way too he ran no risk of being labelled a hobby-horse rider or, more seriously, a persecutor. Throughout the *Grounds and Reasons* he laughed at, reasoned against, and satirized William Whiston's assumption that messianic prophecies in the Old Testament were literally fulfilled in the figure and mission of Jesus. Within two years and in a new work, he substituted Edward Chandler, Bishop of Coventry and Lichfield, for the mathematician. It need not have been the Bishop; any one of thirty-four others could have qualified for the role of opponent, among them people like Clarke, and Sykes, and Sherwood, and even the ubiquitous Whiston. Collins rejected them, however, to debate in the *Scheme* with Bishop Chandler, the author of *A Defence of Christianity from the Prophecies of the Old Testament,* with one who was, in short, the least controversial and yet the most orthodox of his many assailants.

Early in 1727 the Anglican establishment came to the abrupt realization that the subject of the continuing debate—the reliability of the argument from prophecy—was inconclusive, that it could lead only to pedantic wrangling and hair-splitting with each side vainly clutching victory. Certainly the devotion of many clergymen to biblical criticism was secondary to their interest in orthodoxy as a functional adjunct of government, both civil and canonical. It was against this interest, as it was enunciated in Rogers's *Eight Sermons concerning the Necessity of Revelation* (1727) and particularly in its vindictive preface, that Collins chose to fight.[7] The debate had now taken a happy turn for him. As he saw it, the central issue devolved upon man's natural right to religious liberty. At least he made this the theme of his *Letter to Dr. Rogers*. In writing to Des Maizeaux about the success of this work, he obviously enjoyed his own profane irony:

> I have had particular compliments made me by the B^P
> of Salisbury, and by Dr Clark, who among other things
> sayd, that the Archbp of Canterbury might have writ
> all that related to Toleration in it: to say nothing of
> what I hear from others. Dr Rogers himself has acknow-
> ledg[ed] to his Bookseller who sent it to him into the
> Country, that he has receivd it; but says that he is so
> engaged in other affairs, that he has no thought at
> present of answering it; tho he may perhaps in time do
> so.[8]

In time Rogers did. He counterattacked on 2 February 1728 with a *Vindication of the Civil Establishment of Religion*.[9] For Collins this work was a dogged repetition of what had gone before, and so it could be ignored except for one of its appendices, *A Letter from the Rev. Dr. Marshall jun. To the Rev. Dr. Rogers, upon Occasion of his Preface to his Eight Sermons*. Its inclusion seemed an afterthought; yet it altered the dimensions of the debate by narrowing and particularizing the areas of grievance which separated the debaters. Collins, therefore, rebutted it some fourteen months later in *A Discourse concerning Ridicule and Irony in Writing.* He had great hopes for this pamphlet, preparing carefully for its reception. He encouraged the republication of his three preceding works, which find their inevitable conclusion, even their exoneration, in this last performance, and he probably persuaded his bookseller to undertake an elaborate promotional campaign. For the new editions were advertised on seven different days between 10 January and 27 February 1729 in the *Daily Post.* He wanted no one to miss the relationship between the *Discourse concerning Ridicule and Irony* and these earlier pieces or to overlook its presence when it finally appeared in the pamphlet shops on 17 March.

Collins was animated by his many debates. Indeed, "he sought the storms." Otherwise he would not, could not, have participated in these many verbal contests. Throughout them all, his basic strategy—that of provocation—was determined by the very real fact that he had many more enemies than allies, among them, for instance, such formidable antagonists as Swift and Richard Bentley.[10] To survive he had to acquire a tough resilience, a skill in fending off attacks or turning them to his own advantage. Nevertheless, he remained a ready target all his life. Understandably so: his radicalism was stubborn and his opinions predictable. Such firmness may of course indicate his aversion to trimming. Or it may reveal a lack of intellectual growth; what he believed as a young man, he perpetuated as a mature adult. Whether our answer is drawn from either possibility or, more realistically, from both, the fact remains that he never camouflaged the two principles by which he lived and fought:

> 1. That universal liberty be established in respect to opinions and practises not prejudicial to the peace and welfare of society: by which establishment, truth must needs have the advantages over *error* and *false-hood,* the *law* of *God* over the *will* of *man,* and *true Christianity tolerated;* private *judgment* would be really exercised; and men would be allowed to have suffered to follow their consciences, over which God only is supreme: . . .
>
> 2. Secondly, that nothing but the *law of nature,* (the observance whereof is absolutely necessary to society)

and what can be built thereon, should be enforced by
the civil sanctions of the magistrate: . . . [11]

II

There is very little in this statement to offend modern readers.
Yet the orthodox in Collins's own time had reason to be angry with
him: his arguments were inflammatory and his rhetoric was devious,
cheeky, and effective. Those contesting him underscored his nega-
tivism, imaging him as a destroyer of Christianity eager "to pro-
selyte men, from the Christian to no religion at all." [12] Certainly
it is true that he aimed to disprove a Christian revelation which
he judged fraudulent and conspiratorial. In place of ecclesiastical
authority he offered the rule of conscience. For othodoxy he substituted "a Religion antecedent to Revelation, which is necessary
to be known in order to *ascertain Revelation;* and by that Religion
[he meant] *Natural Religion,* which is presupposed to Revelation,
and is a Test by which Reveal'd Religion is to be tried, is a Bot-
tom on which it must stand, and is a Rule to understand it by." [13]
Categorical in tone, the statement frustrated the Anglican clergy
by its very slipperiness; its generalities left little opportunity for
decisive rebuttal. It provided no definition of natural religion beyond the predication of a body of unnamed moral law which is rational and original, the archetype of what is valid in the world's
religions.
    His dismissal of revelation and his reduction of Christianity
to what he called its "natural" and hence incontrovertible basis
carried with it a corollary, that of man's absolute right to religious
enquiry and profession. Here he became specific, borrowing from
Lockean empiricism his conditions of intellectual assent. "Evidence," he said, "ought to be the sole ground of Assent, and Examination is the way to arrive at Evidence; and therefore rather
than I wou'd have Examination, Arguing and Objecting laid aside,
I wou'd chuse to say, That no Opinions whatever can be dangerous
to a Man that impartially examines into the Truth of Things." [14]
The church leadership saw in this statement and others like it not
an epistemological premise but a deliberate subterfuge, an insidious blind to vindicate his attacks upon an organized priesthood.

We can recognize now that his opponents oversimplified his intention, that they blackened it to make his villainy at once definitive and vulnerable. At the same time we must admit that he often equated the ideas of repression and clerical authority, even as he coupled those of freedom and the guide of private conscience.

The Anglican church was infuriated by these correlations, angered as much by their manner of expression as by their substance. For the faithful were frequently thrown off balance by a strategy of ironical indirection. Sometimes this took the form of omission or the presentation of an argument in so fragmentary or slanted a fashion that Collins's "Enemies" could debate neither his implications nor his conclusions. At other times he used this artful circumlocution to create his favorite mask, that of the pious Christian devoted to scripture or of the moralist perplexed by the divisions among the orthodox clergy. Finally, his rhetoric was shaped by deistic predecessors who used sarcasm and satire to mock the gravity of church authority. So much was their wit a trademark that as early as 1702 one commentator had noted, "when you expect an argument, they make a jest." [15] Collins himself resorted to this practice with both instinctive skill and deliberate contrivance.

All these methods, though underhanded, he silently justified on the assumption that he was dealing with a conspiracy of priests: hence, he professed that he had to fight fraud and deception with their like, and that such craftiness, suitable "to his particular genius and temper," was "serviceable to his cause." For these reasons even William Warburton, who had vainly struggled to be judicious, described him as "a Writer, whose dexterity in the arts of Controversy was so remarkably contrasted by his abilities in reasoning and literature, as to be ever putting one in mind of what travellers tell us of the genius of the proper Indians, who, although the veriest bunglers in all the fine arts of manual operation, yet excel everybody in slight of hand and the delusive feats of activity." [16] Whatever may be said of Collins and his achievement, one fact remains constant. He was a brilliant and persistent trickster whose cunning in the techniques of polemic often silenced an opponent with every substantive right to win the debate.

He seized any opportunity to expose the diversity of ethical and theological opinion which set one Anglican divine against another, "to observe"—as Jenkin put it—"how the gladiators in dispute murder the cause between them, while they so fiercely cut and wound one another." For Collins such observation was more than oratorical artifice; it was one of the dogmas of his near-nihilism. He commented once to Des Maizeaux upon the flurry of critics who replied to his statement of necessitarianism in the *Philosophical Inquiry concerning Human Liberty:*

> I was extreamly pleasd with B^P Hoadley, . . . as it was
> upon the true and only point worth disputing with y^e
> Preists, viz whether we the laity are the Calves and
> Sheep of the Preist. And I am not less pleasd to see
> them manage this controversy with ye same vile arts
> against one another, as they always use towards the
> laity. It must open the eyes of a few and convince them,
> that the Preists mean nothing but wealth and power, and
> have not the least . . . . of those qualitys for wch the
> superstitious world admires them.[17]

He applied this principle of divisive attack in *A Discourse of Free-Thinking.* There in fifty-three pages he transparently ridiculed contradictions which hedged three areas of fundamental religious belief: *"The Nature and Attributes of the Eternal Being or God, . . . the Authority of Scriptures, and . . . the Sense of Scripture."* In accordance with one of his favorite tricks—the massing of eminent authority—his exposition rings with hallowed Anglican names: South, Bull, Taylor, Wallis, Carlton, Davenant, Edwards, More, Tillotson, Fowler, Sherlock, Stillingfleet, Sacheverell, Beveridge, Grabe, Hickes, Lesley.[18] What united these men, he insinuated, was not a Christian commitment but a talent to disagree with one another and even to repudiate themselves—as in the case of Stillingfleet. In effect, the entire *Discourse* bubbles with a carelessly suppressed snicker.

The clergy could not readily reply to this kind of incriminating exposure or deny its reality. They therefore overreacted to other judgments that Collins made, particularly to his attacks upon Christian revelation. These they denigrated as misleading, guileful, sinister, contrived, deceitful, insidious, shuffling, covert, subversive. What they objected to was, first, the way in which he reduced the demonstration of Christian revelation to only the "puzzling and perplexing" argument from prophecy, the casual ease with which he ignored or dismissed those other "clear" proofs derived from the miracles of Jesus and the resurrection itself.[19] But even more the orthodox resented the masked point of view from which Collins presented his disbelief.

For example, the *Grounds and Reasons* is the deist's first extended attack upon revelation. Ostensibly it is, as we have seen, an answer to Whiston's *Essay Towards Restoring the True Text of the Old Testament; and for Vindicating the Citations Made Thence in the New Testament* (1722). In it the mathematician argued that the Hebraic prophecies relating to the messiah had been literally fulfilled in Jesus. But this truth, he admitted, had been obscured "in the latter Ages," only because of those "Difficulties" which "have [almost wholly] arisen from the Corruptions, the unbelieving *Jews* introduc'd into the Hebrew and Greek copies of the Old Testament, [soon after] the Beginning of the Second Century." These conspiratorial corruptions he single-handedly planned to remove, returning the Old Testament to a state of textual purity with emendations drawn from sources as varied as the Samaritan Pentateuch, the Greek Psalms, the Antiquities of Josephus, the Chaldee Paraphrases, the books of Philo. His pragmatic purpose was to nullify the biblical criticism of historical minded scholars as reputable as Grotius, to render useless the allegorical interpretation of messianic prophecies. That is, he saw in the latter a "pernicious" absence of fact, a "weak and enthusiastical" whimsy, unchristian adjustments to the exigencies of the moment.[20]

Collins fought not to destroy Whiston's position, which was all too easily destructible, but to undermine the structure, the very "grounds and reasons" with which orthodoxy supported the mysteries of its faith. To do so, he spun a gigantic web of irony controlled by a persona whose complex purpose was concealed by a mien of hyper-righteousness. Here then was one motivated by a fair-mindedness which allowed him to defend his opponent's right of scriptural exegesis even while disagreeing with its approach and its conclusions. Here too was a conservative Christian different from Whiston "and many other great divines; who seem to pay little deference to the books of the New Testament, the text whereof they are perpetually mending in their sermons, commentaries, and writings, to serve purposes; who pretend *we should have more of the true text by being less tenacious of the printed one,* and in consequence thereof, presume to correct by critical *emendations,* serve *capital places* in the *sacred writers;* and who . . . do virtually set aside the authority of the scripture, and place those compositions in its stead." Finally, here was one who, obedient to the spirit of God's revealed word, rejected the fallacy that messianic prophecy had been fulfilled in Christ in any "literal, obvious and primary sense."[21]

But though the persona could not accept Whiston's program, he was not a mere negativist. With growing excitement he argued for allegorical interpretation. At this point the reader discerns that he has been duped, that nowhere has there been a denial of Whiston's charge that the reading of messianic prophecy in a typical or allegorical or secondary sense is "weak and enthusiastical." On the contrary, the reader finds only the damning innuendo that the two methods—the allegorical and the literal—differ from one another not in kind but in degree of absurdity. After being protected for a long time by all the twists and turns of his creator's irony, the persona finally reveals himself for what he is, a man totally insolent and totally without remorse. Never for one moment did he wish to defend the scheme of allegorical prophecy but to attack it. His argument, stripped of its convolutions and pseudo-piety, moves inexorably to a single, negative conclusion. "Christianity pretends to derive itself from Judaism. JESUS appeals to the religious books of the Jews as prophesying of his Mission. None of these Prophecies can be understood of him but in a *typical allegoric* sense. Now that sense is absurd, and contrary to all scholastic rules of interpretation. Christianity, therefore, not being really predicted in the Jewish Writings, is consequently false."[22]

Collins continued his attack upon Christian revelation in the *Scheme.* In the two years which separated this work from the earlier *Grounds and Reasons,* there occurred no change in the author's argument. What does occur, however, is a perceptive if snide elaboration upon the mask. This is in many ways the same persona who barely suppressed his guffaws in the earlier work. Now he is given an added dimension; he is made more decisively rational than his predecessor and therefore more insightful in his knowledge of rhetorical method. As a disciple of certain Protestant polemicists and particularly of Grotius, whose "integrity," "honor," and biblical criticism he supports, he is the empirical-minded Christian who knows exactly why the literalists have failed to persuade the free-thinkers or even to have damaged their arguments. "For if you begin with Infidels by denying to them, what is evident and agreeable to common sense, I think there can be no reasonable hopes of converting or convincing them."[23] The irony is abrasive simply because it unanswerably singles out the great rhetorical failure of orthodoxy, its inability to argue from a set of principles as acceptable to the deists as to themselves.

Many of the clergy chafed against Collins's manipulation of this tongue-in-cheek persona. They resented his irreverent wit which projected, for example, the image of an Anglican God who "talks to all mankind from corners" and who shows his back parts to Moses. They were irritated by his jesting parables, as in "The Case of Free-Seeing," and by the impertinence of labelling Archbishop Tillotson as the man "whom all *English Free-Thinkers* own as their Head."[24]

But most of all they gagged upon Collins's use of satire in religious controversy. As we have already seen, there were complex reasons for his choice of technique. He was a naturally witty man who, sometimes out of fear and sometimes out of malice, expressed himself best through circuitous irony. In 1724, when he himself considered his oratorical practice, he argued that his matter determined his style, that the targets of his belittling wit were the "saint-errants." We can only imagine the exasperation of Collins's Anglican enemies when they found their orthodoxy thus slyly lumped with the eccentricities of Samuel Butler's "true blew" Presbyterians. It would be hard to live down the associations of those facetious lines which made the Augustan divines, like their unwelcome forebear Hudibras, members

> Of that stubborn Crew
> Of Errant Saints, whom all men grant
> To be the true Church Militant.

Those dignified Anglican exteriors were further punctured by Collins's irreverent attack upon their cry of religious uniformity, a cry which was "ridiculous, romantick, and impossible to succeed." He saw himself, in short, as an emancipated Butler or even Cervantes; and like his famous predecessors he too would laugh quite out of countenance the fool and the hypocrite, the pretender and the enthusiast, the knave and the persecuter, all those who would create a god in their own sour and puny image.

III

By 1727 several of the orthodox felt that they could take no more of Collins's laughter, his sneering invectives against the clergy, or his designs to make religion "a Matter purely personal; and the Knowledge of it to be obtain'd by personal Consideration, *independently of any Guides, Teachers, or Authority.*" In the forefront of this group was John Rogers, whose hostility to the deist was articulate and compulsive. At least it drove him into a position seemingly at odds with the spirit if not the law of English toleration. He urged, for example, that those like Collins be prosecuted in a civil court for a persuasion "which is manifestly subversive of all Order and Polity, and can no more consist with civil, than with religious, Society."[25]

Thereupon followed charge and countercharge. New gladiators, as different from each other as the nonconformist divine Samuel Chandler and the deist Thomas Chubb, entered the arena on behalf of Collins. For all the dogmatic volubility of Rogers, orthodoxy appeared beleaguered. The moderate clergy, who witnessed this exchange, became alarmed; they feared that in the melee the very heart of English toleration would be threatened by the contenders, all of whom spoke as its champion. Representative of such moderation was Nathanael Marshall, who wished if not to end the debate, then at least to contain its ardor. As canon of Windsor, he supported the condition of a state religion protected by the magistrate but he worried over the extent of the latter's prerogative and power. Certainly he was more liberal than Rogers in his willingness to entertain professions of religious diversity. Yet he straitjacketed his liberalism when he denied responsible men the right to attack laws, both civil and canonical, with "ludicrous Insult" or "with Buffoonery and Banter, Ridicule or Sarcastick Irony."[26]

Once again Collins met the challenge. In *A Discourse concerning Ridicule and Irony* he devoted himself to undermining the moral, the intellectual, and practical foundations of that one restraint which Marshall would impose upon the conduct of any religious quarrel. He had little difficulty in achieving his objective. His adversary's stand was visibly vulnerable and for several reasons. It was too conscious of the tug-of-war between the deist and Rogers, too arbitrary in its choice of prohibition. It was, in truth, strained by a choice between offending the establishment and yet rejecting clerical extremism.[27] Moreover, Collins had this time an invisible partner, a superior thinker against whom he could test his own ideas and from whom he could borrow others. For the *Discourse concerning Ridicule and Irony* is largely a particularization, a crude but powerful reworking of Shaftesbury's *Sensus Communis: An Essay on the Freedom of Wit and Humour.*

Supported by Shaftesbury's urbane generalization, Collins laughed openly at the egocentricity and blindness of Marshall's timid zealotry. Indeed, he wryly found his orthodox opponent guilty of the very crime with which he, as a subversive, was charged. It seemed to him, he said,

> a most prodigious Banter upon [mankind], for Men to
> talk in general of the *Immorality* of *Ridicule* and *Irony,*
> and of *punishing* Men for those Matters, when their own
> Practice is *universal Irony* and *Ridicule* of all those
> who go not with them, and *universal Applause* and
> *Encouragement* for such *Ridicule* and *Irony,* and dis-
> tinguishing by all the honourable ways imaginable
> such *drolling* Authors for their Drollery; and when
> Punishment for *Drollery* is never call'd for, but when
> *Drollery* is used or employ'd against them!
>
> (p. 29)

Collins's technique continued its ironic ambiguity, reversal, and obliquity. Under a tone of seeming innocence and good will, he credited his adversaries with an enviable capacity for satiric argument. In comradely fashion, he found precedent for his own rhetorical practice through a variety of historical and biblical analogies. But even more important for a contemporary audience, he again resorted to the device of invoking the authority provided by some of the most respected names in the Anglican Establishment. The use of satire in religious topics, hence, was manifest in "the Writings of our most eminent Divines," especially those of Stillingfleet, "our greatest controversial Writer" (pp. 4–5).

With all the outrageous assurance of a self-invited guest, the deist had seated himself at the table of his vainly protesting Christian hosts (whom he insisted on identifying as brethren). "In a word," he said so as to obviate debate, "the Opinions and Practices of Men in all Matters, and especially in Matters of Religion, are generally so absurd and ridiculous that it is impossible for them not to be the Subjects of Ridicule" (p. 19). Thus adopting Juvenal's concept of satiric necessity ("difficile est saturam non scribere"), Collins here set forth the thesis and rationale of his enemy. There was a kind of impudent virtuosity in his "proofs," in his manner of drawing a large, impressive cluster of names into his ironic net and making all of them appear to be credible witnesses in his defense. Even Swift, amusingly compromised as "one of the greatest *Droles* that ever appear'd upon the Stage of the World" (p. 39), was brought to the witness box as evidence of the privileged status to which satiric writing was entitled. Collins enforced erudition with cool intelligence so that contemptuous amusement is present on every page of his *Discourse.*

Beneath his jeers and his laughter there was a serious denunciation of any kind of intellectual restraint, however mild-seeming; beneath his verbal pin-pricking there was conversely an exoneration of man's right to inquire, to profess, and to persuade. Beneath his jests and sarcasms there was further a firm philosophical commitment that informed the rhetoric of all his earlier work. Ridicule, he asserted in 1729, "is both a proper and necessary Method of Discourse in many Cases, and especially in the Case of *Gravity,* when that is attended with Hypocrisy or Imposture, or with Ignorance, or with soureness of Temper and Persecution: all which ought to draw after them the *Ridicule* and *Contempt* of the Society, which has no other effectual Remedy against such

Methods of Imposition" (p. 22).

For the modern reader the *Discourse concerning Ridicule and Irony* is the most satisfactory of Collins's many pamphlets and books. It lacks the pretentiousness of the *Scheme*, the snide convolutions of the *Grounds and Reasons*, the argument by half-truths of the *Discourse of Free-Thinking*. His last work is free of the curious ambivalence which marked so many of his earlier pieces, a visible uncertainty which made him fear repression and yet court it. On the contrary, his last work is in fact a justification of his rhetorical mode and religious beliefs; it is an *apologia pro vita sua* written with all the intensity and decisiveness that such a justification demands. To be sure, it takes passing shots at old enemies like Swift, but never with rancor. And while its language is frequently ironical, its thinking makes an earnest defense of wit as a weapon of truth. The essay sets forth its author as an *animal ridens*, a creature that through laughter and affable cynicism worships a universal God and respects a rational mankind.

Brown University

NOTES TO THE INTRODUCTION

1. *Universal Spectator, and Weekly Journal,* No. 98 (22 August 1730).

2. To Des Maizeaux (5 May 1717): B.M. Sloane MSS. 4282, ff. 129–130.

3. To Des Maizeaux (9 February 1716): B.M. Sloane MSS. 4282, f. 123.

4. The title page of the *Scheme* is dated 1726. It was not advertised in the newspapers or journals of that year—a strange silence for any of Collins's work. Its first notice appeared in the *Monthly Catalogue: Being a General Register of Books, Sermons, Plays, Poetry, Pamphlets, &c. Printed and Publish'd in London, or the Universities, during the Month of May, 1727* (see No. 49). Yet we know that the *Scheme* had been remarked upon as early as March when on the 10th of that month Samuel Chandler published his *Reflections on the Conduct of the Modern Deists in their late Writings against Christianity.* (For the dating of Chandler's work, see the *Daily Courant* ⌊10 March 1727⌋.) We know also that the *Scheme* went to a second edition late in 1727 and was frequently advertised in the *Daily Post* between 2 January and 20 January 1728.

5. For the statement about the *Letter to Dr. Rogers,* see B. M. Sloane MSS. 4282, f. 220 (15 August 1727). For that on the use of "personal matters" in controversy, see B. M. Sloane MSS. 4282, f. 170 (27 December 1719); cf. *The Scheme of Literal Prophecy Considered* (London, 1726), pp. 422–438.

6. *The Grounds and Reasons of the Christian Religion* was published in London within the first four days of January 1724; see the advertisement in the *Daily Post* (4 January 1724). *A Discourse concerning Ridicule and Irony in Writing* was published on or close to 17 March 1729; see the advertisement in the *Daily Journal* for that date.

7. We can generally fix the date of Rogers's *Eight Sermons* within the first two months of 1727 because it was answered early by Samuel Chandler's *Reflections on the Conduct of the Modern Deists.* (See note 4.) For the dating of Collins's rebuttal, see the *Monthly Catalogue,* No. 49 (May 1727).

8. To Des Maizeaux (24 June 1727): B.M. Sloane MSS. 4282, ff. 218–219.

9. For the dating of this work, see the *Daily Post* (31 January 1728).

10. For Swift's satire, see *Mr. C---ns's Discourse of Free-Thinking,
Put into plain English, by way of Abstract, for the Use of the Poor.*
For Bentley's devastating probe of Collins's scholarly inadequacies,
see his *Remarks on the Discourse of Free-Thinking. By Phileleu-
therus Lipsiensis.* Both works appeared in 1713.

11. *Scheme,* pp. 432—433.

12. Edward Chandler, *A Defence of Christianity from the Prophecies of
the Old Testament* (London, 1725), p. ii.

13. *A Letter to Dr. Rogers,* p. 89.

14. *A Vindication of the Divine Attributes* (London, 1710), p. 24.

15. Robert Jenkin, *A Brief Confutation of the Pretences against Natural
and Revealed Religion* (London, 1702), p. 40.

16. For Collins on his own rhetorical skills, see *Scheme,* p. 402; William
Warburton, *Divine Legation of Moses, Demonstrated* (London, 1846),
III, 199.

17. Jenkin, *Brief Confutation,* p. 51; for the letter (1 July 1717), see
B. M. Sloane MSS. 4282, f. 137.

18. Pp. 46—99.

19. See, for example, the statement of John Conybeare, Bishop of Bristol,
in Joseph Spence, *Observations, Anecdotes, and Characters of Books
and Men,* ed. James M. Osborn (Oxford, 1966), I, sect. 992.

20. *Essay,* pp. 329—333 (for Whiston's statement of sources); pp. 334—335
(for his defense of literal interpretation). The bracketed material
indicates Whiston's manuscript emendations of his own printed text;
see the British Museum's copy of the *Essay* (873. 1. 10) which originally belonged to the mathematician. See Collins, *Grounds and
Reasons,* pp. 98—99, for the summary of Whiston's attack upon allegorical interpretation.

21. *Grounds and Reasons,* pp. 20, 48—50.

22. This terse summary of the persona's argument was correctly made
by Warburton, III, 232.

23. *Scheme,* p. 391.

24. *Discourse of Free-Thinking,* pp. 15—17, 38, 171.

25. *Eight Sermons,* pp. 1, lxi.

26. Marshall, pp. 301, 337. For Samuel Chandler's contribution, see his *Reflections on the Conduct of the Modern Deists* (London, 1727); for Chubb's contribution see *Some Short Reflections on the Grounds and Extent of Authority and Liberty, With respect to the Civil Government* (London, 1728).

27. Marshall's reluctance to support Rogers's extremism is seen in the funeral sermon he preached at the latter's death (*A Sermon Delivered in the Parish Church of St. Giles Cripplegate, May 18, 1729. Upon Occasion of the Much Lamented Death of the Rev^d. John Rogers* [London, 1729]). He made only the most casual and indifferent reference to Rogers's work. So obvious was this slight that it called for a rebuttal; see Philalethes (A. A. Sykes [?]), *Some Remarks Upon the Reverend Dr. Marshall's Sermon on Occasion of the Death of the Revd Dr Rogers* (London, 1729).

BIBLIOGRAPHICAL NOTE

This facsimile of *A Discourse concerning Ridicule and Irony in Writing* (1729) is reproduced from a copy in the William Andrews Clark Memorial Library.

A

DISCOURSE

CONCERNING

Ridicule and Irony

IN

WRITING,

IN A

LETTER

To the Reverend

Dr. NATHANAEL MARSHALL.

——————— *Ridiculum acri*
Fortius & melius magnas plerumq; fecat res.

——————— *Ridentem dicere verum*
Quid vetat?

LONDON:

Printed for J. BROTHERTON in *Cornhill*, and fold
by T. WARNER in *Pater-nofter-Row*, and
A. DODD without *Temple-Bar*. 1729.

A

DISCOURSE

CONCERNING

Ridicule and *Irony*, &c.

REVEREND SIR,

IN your *Letter* to Dr. *Rogers*, which he has publifh'd at the End of his *Vindication of the Civil
Eftablifhment of Religion*, I find a Notion
advanc'd by you : which as it is a common
and plaufible Topick for Perfecution, and a Topick by which you, and many others, urge the
Magiftrate to punifh [or, as you phrafe it, *to pinch*]
* Men for controverfial Writings, is particularly
proper at this time to be fully confider'd ; and I
hope to treat it in fuch manner as to make you your
felf, and every fair Reader, fenfible of the Weaknefs thereof.

  You profefs to " vindicate † a fober, ferious,
" and modeft Inquiry into the Reafons of any Efta-
" blifhment."

* *Page* 337.   † *Pag.* 302.

(4)

And you add, that you " have not ordinarily " found it judg'd inconsistent with the Duty of a " *private Subject*, to propose his Doubts or his Rea- " sons to the Publick in a *modest* way, concerning " the *Repeal* of any Law which he may think of " ill Consequence by its Continuance. If he be a " Man of Ability, and well vers'd in the Argu- " ment, he will deserve some Attention; but if " he mistakes his Talent, and will be busy with " what he very little understands, Contempt and " Odium will be his unavoidable and just Allot- " ment." And you say, that " Religion is more " a personal Affair, in which every Man has a pe- " culiar Right and Interest, and a Concern that " he be not mistaken, than in any other Case or " Instance which can fall under the Cognizance of " the Magistrate; and that greater Allowances " seem due to each private Person for Examination " and Inquiry in this, than in any other Example."

And herein I must do you the Justice to acknow- ledge, that you speak like a Christian, like a Protestant, like an *Englishman*, and a reasonable Man; like a Man concerned for Truth, like a Man of Conscience; like a Man concern'd for the Consciences of others; like a Man concern'd to have some Sense, Learn- ing, and Virtue in the World; and, in a word, like a Man who is not for abandoning all the va- luable Things in Life to the Tyranny, Ambition, and Covetousness of Magistrates and Ecclesiasticks.

But you observe, that " municipal Laws *, how " trivial soever in their intrinsick Value, are never " to be *insulted*; never to be treated with *Buffoonery* " and *Banter*, *Ridicule* and *sarcastick Irony*. So " that Dr. *Rogers*'s grand Adversary will have from " you no measure of Encouragement to his man- " ner of Writing." Again, you " never † desire " to see the Magistrate fencing in the publick Re-

* *Page* 201.   † *Pag.* 307.

" ligion

" ligion with fo thick a Hedge as fhall exclude
" all Light, and fhall tear out the Eyes of all fuch
" as endeavour to fee thro' it. *Sober arguing* you
" never fear : *Mockery* and *bitter Railing*, if you
" could help it, you would never bear, either
" *for the Truth or againft it*."

Upon which I offer thefe following Confiderations.

1. *Firft*, If what you call *Infult*, *Buffoonery*,
Banter, *Ridicule* and *Irony*, *Mockery* and *bitter Railing*, be Crimes in Difputation, you will find none
more deeply involv'd in it than our moft famous
Writers, in their controverfial Treatifes about *ferious* Matters ; as all Notions and Practices in Religion, whether reafonable or abfurd, may be equally
and juftly deem'd : the Notions and Practices of
Papifts, Prefbyterians, Quakers, and all other Sects,
being no lefs *ferious* to their refpective Sects than ridiculous to one another. Let any Man read the Writings
of our moft eminent Divines againft the *Papifts*, *Puritans*, *Diffenters*, and *Hereticks*, and againft one another, and particularly the Writings of *Alexander
Cook*, *Hales*, *Chillingworth*, *Patrick*, *Tillotfon*, *Stillingfleet*, *Burnet*, *South*, *Hickes*, *Sherlock* and *Edwards*, and he will find them to abound with *Banter*,
Ridicule, and *Irony*. *Stillingfleet* in particular, our
greateft controverfial Writer, who paffes for *grave*
and *folemn*, is fo confcious of his ufe thereof, that he
confeffes that Charge of the Papifts againft him,
faying *, " But I forget my Adverfary's grave ad-
" monition, that I *would treat thefe Matters ferioufly,
" and lay afide Drollery*." And again, after a *Banter*
of near a Page, he fays †, " But I forget I am fo
" near my Adverfary's Conclufion, wherein he fo
" *gravely* advifes me, that I *would be pleas'd for once*

---

* Stillingfleet's *Anfwer to feveral late Treatifes*, &c. *Page*
14. † *Pag.* 71.

A 3   " *to*

" *to write Controverſy, and not Play-Books.*" Nor
did I ever hear the Divines of the Church condemn
the Doctor for his ſarcaſtical Method of writing
Controverſy. On the contrary, I remember at the
Univerſity, that he uſed to be applauded no leſs for
his Wit than for his Learning. And to exalt his
Character as a Wit, his *Conferences between a* Ro-
miſh *Prieſt, a Fanatick Chaplain, and a Divine of the
Church of* England, *&c.* were ſpoken of as an excellent *Comedy,* and eſpecially for that Part which the
Fanatick Chaplain acts therein, who makes as comical and as ridiculous a Figure as he does in any of the
Plays acted on the Stage. And in his *Controverſy*
with *Dryden* about the *Royal Papers,* and thoſe of
the *Duchess* of *York,* he was deem'd to have out-
done that famous *Satiriſt* in tart Repartees and Reflections ; and to have attack'd the Character of the
Poet with more ſeverity, than that *Poet,* who was ſo
remarkable for his ſatirical Reflections on the holy
Order, did the Character of the *Divine :* As for
example, he ſays to *Dryden* *, " Could nothing be
" ſaid by you of Biſhop *Morley,* but that *Prelate*
" *of rich Memory ?* Or had you a mind to tell us
" he was no *Poet ?* Or that he was out of the
" Temptation of changing his Religion for
" Bread ?" And many Citations us'd to be produc'd
out of his Writings, as Specimens of his ironical
Talent ; among which I particularly remember his
Ridicule of his Adverſary Mr. *Alſop,* a famous Preſ-
byterian Wit and Divine ; whoſe Book, which was
full of low Raillery and Ridicule, he reſembles † to
the Bird of Athens, as *made up of Face and Feathers.*
And the Doctor himſelf adds, in Juſtification of
the polite Method of Raillery in Controverſy, that
there is a pleaſantneſs of Wit, which ſerves to entertain

---

† Vindication of the Anſwer to the Royal Papers. *p.* 105.
‡ *Preface to* Unreaſonableneſs of Separation. *p.* 62.

the

the Reader in the rough and deep way of Controversy.
Nor did Mr. *Alsop* want Approvers of his Raillery
in his own Party. Mr. *Gilbert Rule* [*], a great *Scotch*
Presbyterian Divine, who defended him against
Stillingfleet, contends in behalf of his Raillery,
" That the Facetiousness of Mr. *Alsop*'s Strain
" needed to have bred no Disgust, being as a
" Condiment to prevent *Tædium* and Nauseousness."
And he adds, " That he knows none that blame
" the excellent Writings of Mr. *Fuller*, which have
" a Pleasantness not unlike that of Mr. *Alsop*."

And this manner of writing is seldom complain'd
of, as unfit to be allow'd, by any but those who feel
themselves hurt by it. For the solemn and grave
can bear a solemn and grave Attack: That gives
them a sort of Credit in the World, and makes
them appear considerable to themselves, as worthy
of a serious Regard. But *Contempt* is what they,
who commonly are the most contemptible and
worthless of Men, cannot bear nor withstand, as
setting them in their true Light, and being the most
effectual Method to drive Imposture, the sole Foun-
dation of their Credit, out of the World. Hence
Stillingfleet's Popish Adversaries, more conscious
perhaps of the Ridiculousness of Popery than the
common People among Protestants themselves, fall
upon him very furiously. One says [†], " That by
" the Phrases, which are the chief Ornaments that
" set off the Doctor's Works, we may easily guess
" in what Books he has spent his Time; and that
" he is well vers'd in *Don Quixot*, the *Seven Cham-*
" *pions*, and other *Romantick Stories*. Sure the
" Doctor err'd in his Vocation: Had he quitted
" all serious Matters, and dedicated himself wholly
" to Drollery and Romance, with two or three

---

[*] Rule's *Rational Defence of* Nonconf. *p.* 29.
[†] *Preface to* Stillingfleet *still against* Stillingfleet.

" Y

" Years under *Hudibras*, he might have been a
" Mafter in that Faculty ; the Stage might have
" been a Gainer by it, and the Church of *England*
" would have been no Lofer."

Another of his Adverfaries fays, " * Perufe the
" Doctor Page after Page, you will find the Man
" all along in peevifh Humour, when you fee his
" Book brimfull of tart biting Ironies, Drolleries,
" comical Expreffions, impertinent Demands, and
" idle Stories, &c. as if the difcharging a little
" Gall were enough to difparage *the cleareft Mi-*
" *racles* God ever wrought."

But what are thefe *cleareft Miracles God ever*
wrought ? Why, the moft extravagant, whimfical,
abfurd, and ridiculous Legends and Stories imaginable ; fuch as that of *St. Dominick* †, who when
the Devil came to him in the Shape of a *Monkey*,
made him hold a Candle to him while he wrote,
and keep it fo long between his Toes, till it burnt
them ; and his keeping the Devil, who fometimes
came to him in the Shape of a *Flea*, and by fkip-
ping on the Leaves of his Book difturb'd his Reading, in that Shape, and ufing him for a Mark to
know where he left off reading : Such as St. *Pa-*
trick's heating an Oven with Snow, and turning a
Pound of Honey into a Pound of Butter : Such as
Chrift's marrying Nuns, and playing at Cards with
them ; and Nuns living on the Milk of the bleffed
Virgin *Mary* ; and that of divers Orders, and efpecially the *Benedictine*, being fo dear to the bleffed
Virgin, that in Heaven fhe lodges them under her
Petticoats : Such as making broken Eggs whole ;

---

* *Preface to a Difcourfe of* Miracles wrote in the *Roman*
Church, &c.

† See *Stillingfleet's* Second Vind. of the Proteftant Grounds
of Faith, c. 3.

and

and of People, who had their Heads cut off, walking with their Heads in their Hands, which were fometimes fet on again: Such as Fafting for a hundred Years ; and raifing Cows, Calves, and Birds from the Dead, after they had been chopt to Pieces and eaten, and putting on their Heads after they had been pull'd or cut off ; and turning a Pound of Butter into a Bell ; and making a Bull give Milk ; and raifing a King's Daughter from the Dead, and turning her into a Son ; and the feveral Tranflations thro' the Air of the Virgin *Mary*'s Houfe from *Palcfline* to *Loretto*, and the Miracles wrote there ; and more of the like Kind.

Are thefe, or fuch as thefe the *cleareft Miracles God ever wrought?* Do fuch Miracles deferve a ferious Regard? And fhall the *Gravity* with which Mankind is thus banter'd out of their common Senfe, excufe thefe Matters from *Ridicule?*

It will be difficult to find any Writers who have exceeded the Doctors, *South* and † *Edwards*, in *Banter, Irony, Satire* and *Sarcafms:* The laft of whom has written a Difcourfe in *Defence of fharp Reflections on Authors and their Opinions* ; wherein he enumerates, as Examples for his Purpofe, almoft all the eminent Divines of the Church of *England.* And Mr. ‡ *Collier,* fpeaking of a Letter of the Venerable *Bede* to *Egbert* Bifhop of *York,* fays, " The Satire and Declamation in this *Epiftle* fhews " the *pious Zeal* and *Integrity* of the Author ;" which feems to imply, that *Satire* and *Declamation* is the orthodox and moft pious Method of writing in behalf of *Orthodoxy.*

---

† *Edwards*'s New Difcov. *p.* 184—215.
‡ *Ecclefiaft. Hift.* cent. 8. *p.* 196.

Dr. *Rogers*, to whom you write, falls into the
Method of Buffoonery, Banter, Satire, Drollery,
Ridicule, and Irony, even in the Treatife to which
your Letter is fubjoined, and againft that *Perfon*
whom you would have punifh'd for that Method :
When he fays to him, * " Religion then, it
" feems, muft be left to the Scholars and Gentle-
" folks, and to them 'tis to be of no other ufe, but
" as a Subject of Difputation to improve their
" Parts and Learning ; but methinks the Vul-
" gar might be indulged a little of it now and
" then, upon Sundays and Holidays, inftead of
" Bull-baiting and Foot-ball." And this infipid
Piece of Drollery and falfe Wit [which is defign'd
to ridicule his Adverfary for afferting, that *What
Men underftand nothing of, they have no Concern a-
bout*; which is a Propofition that will ftand the
Teft of *Ridicule*, which will be found wholly to lie
againft the Doctor, for afferting the Reafonablenefs
of impofing Things on the People which they do
not underftand] is the more remarkable, as it pro-
ceeds from one, who is at the fame time for ufing
the Sword of the Magiftrate againft his Adverfary.
One would think the † *Inquifitor* fhould banifh
the *Droll*, and the *Droll* the *Inquifitor*.

One of the greateft and beft Authorities for the
pleafant and *ironical* manner of treating *ferious* Matters, is that eminent Divine at the Time of the Reformation, the great *Erafmus*, who has written two
Books in this way with great Applaufe of Pro-
teftants, and without fubjecting himfelf to any Perfecution of Papifts : which makes it highly proper
to propofe them to the Confideration of the Reader, that he may regulate his Notions, by what, it

* Vind. *p.* 199.
† *See* Shaftefbury's *Charactteriflicks*, Vol. I. p. 61.

may

may be prefum'd, he approves of in that Author. Thefe two Books of *Erafmus* are his *Colloquies*, and his *Praife of Folly*.

His *Colloquies* were wrote in imitation of *Lucian's Dialogues*; and I think with equal, if not fuperior, Succefs.

Both thefe Authors had an Averfion to fullen, auftere, defigning Knaves; and both of them being Men of Wit and Satire, employ'd their Talents againft *Superftition* and *Hypocrify*. *Lucian* liv'd in an Age when *Fiction* and *Fable* had ufurp'd the Name of *Religion*, and *Morality* was corrupted by *Men* of *Beard* and *Grimace*, but fcandaloufly *Leud* and *Ignorant*; who yet had the Impudence to preach up *Virtue*, and ftyle themfelves *Philofophers*, perpetually clafhing with one another about the Precedence of their feveral Founders, the Merits of their different Sects, and if 'tis poffible, about Trifles of lefs Importance: yet all agreeing in a different way to dupe and amufe the poor People, by the *fantaftick* Singularity of their Habits, the unintelligible Jargon of their Schools, and their Pretenfions to a fevere and mortify'd Life.

Thefe Jugglers and Impoftors *Lucian* in great meafure help'd to chafe out of the World, by expofing them in their proper Colours, and by reprefenting them as ridiculous as they were. But in a few Generations after him, a new Race of Men fprung up in the World, well known by the Name of *Monks* and *Fryars*, different indeed from the former in Religion, Garb, and a few other Circumftances; but in the main, the fame fort of Impoftors, the fame ever-lafting Cobweb-Spinners, as to their nonfenfical Controverfies, the fame abandon'd *Wretches*, as to their Morals; but as to the myfterious Arts of heaping up Wealth, and picking

the

the People's Pockets, infinitely fuperior to the *Pagan Philofophers* and *Priefts.* Thefe were the fanctify'd Cheats, whofe Folly and Vices *Erafmus* has fo effectually lafh'd, that fome Countries have entirely turn'd thefe Drones out of their Cells ; and in other Places, where they are ftill kept up, they are in fome meafure become contemptible, and obliged to be always on their Guard.

The Papifts fay, that thefe " * *Colloquies,* by turn-
" ing into *Ridicule* the Devotion to the holy Vir-
" gin and Saints, the Worfhip of Relicks and Ima-
" ges, religious Vows and Pilgrimages, have made
" more Hereticks than the Works of *Luther* and
" *Calvin."* And I find the reverend Mr. *Trapp*
[after calling † *Reliques,* F o o l i s h] celebrates *E-
rafmus* for *baving abundantly* R I D I C U L'D *them.*

His *Praife of Folly* treats of *ferious* Matters, in fuch a gay, familiar, ingenious and pleafant manner, as makes it a Work proper to be read by intelligent People, to remove out of their Minds all Bigotry contracted by Ignorance and an evil Education, all Peevifhnefs, Hatred, and Ill-nature towards one another, on account of different Sentiments in Religion ; and to form in them the natural Principles of Moderation, Humanity, Affection and Friendfhip. Our learned and ingenious Bifhop *Kennet* could not do a more fignal Piece of Service to our Country, than by tranflating into *Englifh* this Book, which the Ladies have now an Opportunity of underftanding no lefs than the Men ; and from whence they may fee the pleafant, amiable, and juft Difpofition of Mind of one of the moft learned and ingenious Men that ever liv'd, as well

---

* Memoirs de Trevoux, *An.* 1707. *p.* 396. *An.* 1717.
p. 1200.
† *Trap*'s Popery truly ftated, *p.* 123.

as Author of a great Number of religious and de-
votional Books; nor could the Bishop well give a
heartier Stroke at Popery, than by approving
of *Erasmus's* * *laughing* at it, and applauding his
numberless *Taunts on its Impostures, Cheats, and
Delusions.*

Our Clergy have ever treated Mr. *Hobbes* with
the greatest Mockery, Ridicule and Raillery: As
for example, *Ward* Bishop of *Sarum, Bramhal* Bishop of *Derry, Parker* Bishop of *Oxford,* Dr. *Wallis*
in his several bantering Treatises against him, *Lucy*
Bishop of *St.Davids,Shafto,* and particularly the Reverend *Droll,* Dr. *Eachard,* in two *Dialogues,* which,
it is well known, have been universally well receiv'd by the Clergy, and that for their Treatment
of Mr. *Hobbes* in the ridiculing Way ; for which
the Author himself makes the following just Apology, in his *Dedication* of his *Second Dialogue* to
Archbishop *Sheldon,* " That of all Triflers, 'tis
" the *Set,* the *Grave,* the *Philosophical,* and the
" *Mathematical Trifler,* to which he has the great-
" est Aversion; whom when he meets, very grave-
" ly making out all Men to be rational Beasts
" both in Nature and Conversation, and every
" Man, he pleases, a rational Rebel ; and upon
" any Fright or Pinch a rational Atheist and Anti-
" Christian ; and all this perform'd with all DE-
" MURENESS, SOLEMNITY, QUOTATION
" of SCRIPTURE, APPEALS to CONSCIENCE
" and CHURCH-HISTORY; he must humbly
" beg his *Grace's* Pardon, if then he has endea-
" vour'd to SMILE a little, and to get as much
" out of his Road and way of Writing as possible."
These *Dialogues* used to be much recommended to
the Youth to make them laugh at Mr *Hobbes,* who

---

* *Preface.*

was conftantly reprefented as provok'd and put out
of all Temper by them, and was faid to have vented this ftrange and impious Expreffion, upon its
being told him, that *the Clergy faid* Eachard *had
crucify'd* Hobbes; " Why then don't they fall
" down and worfhip me?"

Mr. *Selden* has been the conftant Subject of Clergy-
banter, for his *Hiftory of Tythes*; in the *Preface* to
which, " He reproaches the Clergy with Igno-
" rance and Lazinefs, and upbraids them with hav-
" ing nothing to keep up their Credit but *Beard,*
" *Title,* and *Habit;* and their Studies reach'd no
" farther than the *Breviary,* the *Poftils,* and *Poly-
" anthea.*" For this Work he was attack'd more
particularly by three Divines, *Tilleſly, Mountagu,*
and *Nettles.* And their Succefs was thus originally
reprefented *, " That he was fo gall'd by *Tilleſly,*
" fo gagg'd by *Mountagu,* and fo ftung by *Nettles,*
" that he never came off in any of his Undertakings
" with more lofs of Credit." And this Jeft has
pafs'd much upon the World, and been continued
down in many Books, where Mr. *Selden* is mention'd, to his Difcredit with ignorant Readers, but
not with the Knowing and Learned; who, as Dr.
Wotton tells us †, *have, now Party-heats are over,*
acquiefced in what Mr. Selden *advanc'd; who
firft,* OF ALL CHRISTIANS, *fet the Affair* of
Tythes *in a clear Light.*

It is ufually faid the Comedy called *Ignoramus,*
which is a Clergy-banter upon the *Law,* was a defign'd Return for Mr. *Selden's Hiftory of Tythes.*

The Reverend Dr. *Beaumont,* late Mafter of St.
Peter's College and King's Profeffor of Divinity, has
given us a Book, entitled, " Some Obfervations

---

* *Heylin's* Hiftory of the Presbyterians, *p.* 391.
† *Wotton* on the *Mifna,* p. 118.

" upon

" upon the Apology of Dr. *Henry More* for his
" *Myftery of Godlinefs* ;" which endeavours to render the faid Doctor *ridiculous*, and fet People a *laughing* at him, (*p. 9. &c.* 64.) and ufed to be applauded
as a complete Performance in the way of Raillery
and Irony, and was well receiv'd for being directed againft a Perfon efteem'd Heterodox.

Many Clergymen have written Books to banter
the Works of Mr. *Locke*, among whom Dr. *Ed-
wards* muft have the firft Place ; whofe *Brief Vindi-
cation of the fundamental Articles of the Chriftian
Faith*, which has the *Imprimatur* before it of *James,
Beaumont, Covel*, and *Balderfton*, four *Cambridge*
Heads, was never exceeded by the moft licentious
Droll.

When *Sorbier*'s *Voyage* to *England*, which was a
pert and infolent Abufe and Satire on the Nation,
and written in the *French* manner of contemptuoufly
treating all Countries and Men but *France* and
Frenchmen, was publifh'd, it was deem'd proper that a drolling and fatirical Anfwer fhould be
given to it, and that the Reverend Dr. *Sprat* fhould
be the *Droll* employ'd; who perform'd his Part
according to the Expectation of the Drolling Court
of King *Charles* II. and as the ingenious Mr. *Addifon*
tells us, * *Vindicated the Honour of his Country, in a
Book full of Satire and Ingenuity.*

Bifhop *Beveridge* ever pafs'd for a ferious and profound Divine ; and his Writings have fix'd that
Character upon him among the Religious of the
High Church, who have receiv'd his *Private
Thoughts* and his Volumes of *Sermons*, like *Manna*
from Heaven. And yet poffibly never Man had
two more fevere Attacks made upon him than he
had ; one by Bifhop *Stillingfleet*, who in *A Vindication of their Majefties Authority to fill the Sees of*

the depriv'd Bishops, &c. occasion'd by Dr. *Beveridge's* Refusal of the Bishoprick of *Bath* and *Wells,* satirizes both his *Prudence* and his *Sincerity;* and another, by an ingenious Bishop also, who in *A short View of Dr.* Beveridge*'s Writings,* has in a most refin'd *drolling manner* reprefented thofe Writings as abounding in moft abfurd and ridiculous Divinity.

But one of the jufteft and fineft Pieces of *Irony,* and the moft timely and feafonably vented, and that deferves perpetual Remembrance, is, *Andrews* the grave Bifhop of *Winchefter's* Irony, on *Neal* the grave Bifhop of *Durham* ; of which we have the following Relation in the Poet *Waller's Life,* prefix'd before his Works : " On the Day of the " Diffolution of the laft Parliament of King *James* " the Firft, Mr. *Waller,* out of Curiofity or Re- " fpect, went to fee the King at Dinner ; with " whom were Dr. *Andrews* the Bifhop of *Win-* " *chefter,* and Dr. *Neal* Bifhop of *Durham,* ftand- " ing behind his Majefty's Chair. There happen'd " fomething very extraordinary in the Converfation " thofe Prelates had with the King, on which " Mr. *Waller* did often reflect. His Majefty afk'd " the Bifhops, *My Lords, cannot I take my Subjects* " *Money when I want it, without all this Formality in* " *Parliament ?* The Bifhop of *Durham* readily " anfwer'd, *God forbid, Sir, but you should; you are* " *the Breath of our Noftrils.* Whereupon the King " turn'd and faid to the Bifhop of *Winchefter,* " *Well, my Lord, what fay you ? Sir,* replied the " Bifhop, *I have no Skill to judge of Parliamentary* " *Cafes.* The King anfwer'd, *No Put-offs, my* " *Lord; anfwer me prefently. Then, Sir,* faid he, " *I think it is lawful for you to take my Brother* Neal*'s* " *Money, for he offers it.* Mr. *Waller* faid the " Company was pleas'd with this Anfwer, and the

" Wit

" Wit of it seem'd to affect the King." Which
shews the exceeding Aptness and Usefulness of a
good *Irony* ; that can convey an Instruction to a
vicious, evil, and tyrannical Prince, highly reflecting on his Conduct, without drawing on his Re-
sentment.

To these famous Divines I might add the most
eminent and renowned Philosophers of Antiquity,
who, either out of a Contempt of Mankind, or to
gratify their peculiar Tempers, or to correct the
Vices and Follies of Men, and to instil virtuous
Maxims in those who would only receive them in
some pleasant way, set up for good Humour,
Mirth, and Drollery, as their standing Method of
Life, and of Conversation with the World ; and
have left behind them some of their occasional
Sayings upon record, which do more Honour to
their Memories than the most elaborate Treatises
would have done, and more Good to Men ; upon
whom a Jest, or witty Saying, is more fitted
to operate and make Impression than long Deducti-
ons and Reasonings, and particularly on Princes and
great Men, who will receive no Instruction but in
some very artful and short Way : whereof even the
rude *Diogenes*, the *Cynick*, has given us a most incomparable Example, in his occasional Conference
with *Alexander the Great*, who was put into such
Temper by the mere Freedom and Raillery of the
Philosopher, as to take every thing in good part he
said to him, and consequently be dispos'd to reflect
upon it, and to act with Discretion. At the Head
of these Philosophers I place S o c r a t e s, who has
very generally in all Ages pass'd for the *wisest* of
Men, and was declared so by an *Oracle* ; which, at
least, was therein directed and influenc'd by some
considerable human Authority, or by the common
Sentiments of Men at that time. His Character I

shall

fhall give you in the words of the moft ingenious *Addifon*, who was himfelf a Mafter of *Humour* and *Drollery*, and practis'd them in Perfection, and with great Succefs in almoft all his Profe-writings. " *Socrates*, fays he *, who was the greateft Propa- " gator of Morality in the Heathen World, and a " Martyr for the Unity of the Godhead, was fo " famous for the exercife of the Talent [of Raillery " and Humour] among the politeft People of An- " tiquity, that he gain'd the Name of T H E " D R O L E.‖" A Character that intitled him to the greateft Merit, as it moft of all enabled him to promote Virtue.

I might alfo offer to your Confideration the Affair of *Comedies* ; which all polite Governments have permitted, or eftablifh'd, in their feveral populous and wealthy Cities, as the neceffary and proper means to encounter Vice and recommend Virtue, and to employ innocently and ufefully the vacant Hours of many, who know not how to em- ploy their Time, or would employ it amifs, by entering into † Factions and Cabals to difturb the State ; or by Gaming, or by backbiting Conver- fations about their Neighbours. And as *Come- dies*, which were originally very grofs, grew by Ufe more polite and refin'd in *Satire* and *Raillery :* fo the moft celebrated Wits and Statefmen, and· Perfons of the greateft Quality, have engag'd and join'd with others in them, and perform'd with the greateft Succefs and Reputation to themfelves ; and have been valu'd, not only for their Talents of *Irony* and *Drollery*, which were effential to the Cre- dit of fuch Performances ; but applauded, as acting the virtuous Part of *Droles*.

* *Freeholder*, Numb. xlv.
‖ *See* Cicero de Officiis, *l.* 1. *c.* 30.
† *See* Patrick's *Friendly Debate*, Part I. *p.* 139~141. *5th Edit.*

In

In fine, Books of Satire, Wit, Humour, Ridi-
dicule, Drollery, and Irony, are the moſt read
and applauded of all Books, in all Ages, Lan-
guages, and Countries. And as thoſe which are
exquiſite in their kinds, are the ſtanding Entertainment of the Ingenious and Learned ; ſo others,
of a lower kind, are to be found among the lower
Readers, who ſleep under all Works which do not
make them merry.

In a word, the Opinions and Practices of Men
in all Matters, and eſpecially in Matters of Religion,
are generally ſo abſurd and ridiculous that it is im-
poſſible for them not to be the Subjects of Ridicule.

For what elſe can be expected from Men who
generally take up their Opinions without any Inquiry into their Reaſonableneſs or Truth, and upon
the moſt incompetent Grounds? I cannot be ſuppoſed to injure Mankind, if I conſider them under
the Character which the very ingenious Sir *Richard
Steele* gives of himſelf ; who *acknowledges* * that (even
while he took upon himſelf the Title of the *Cenſor*
of *Great Britain*, and in ſo many fine Papers cor-
rects his Countrymen, and particularly *the Free-
thinkers*, whom he directs the Magiſtrate to puniſh
with Death) *it had been with him, as it is with too
many others, that a* * *ſort of an* implicit Religion
*ſeem'd the moſt eaſy and moſt comfortable ; and that a
blind Veneration for* he knew not what, *and he* knew
not whom, *ſtood for every thing important.* And he
*confeſſes he was not enough aware, that this Implicitneſs
of Conduct is the great Engine of Popery, fram'd for
the Deſtruction of* good Nature, *as well as* good
Senſe. If ſo great a Man could take up with ſuch
a Method, and act the Part of a *Cenſor* and Di-

* *Preface to* The State of the Roman Catholick Religion,
p. 11.

rector

rector of others, in a Matter which he had not at all confider'd, what can be expected elfe from others, but abfurd and ridiculous Opinions and Practices ?

And if fome Men will fall into abfurd and ridiculous Opinions, Habits, Forms, Figures and Grimaces; there will be thofe who will *laugh*, nay, cannot help *laughing* at them. Hence moft Parties laugh at one another, without the leaft Scruple, and with great Applaufe of their own Parties ; and the Leaders of the fame Party laugh with one another, when they confider the abfurd and ridiculous Opinions they profefs, and how they cheat and govern their Followers ; agreeably to what *Cicero* reports of *Cato* *, " *Vetus autem illud* Catonis " *admodum fcitum eft, qui* mirari fe *aiebat, quod non* " *rideret haruspex cum haruspicem vidiffet.*"

I think it may be juftly fuppos'd, that Pope *Alexander* and *Thomas Becket* could not but laugh together at the Simplicity and Weaknefs of their Followers, the Papifts, who receiv'd for truth the following Story. It was told as a Fact †, " that " when *Thomas Becket*, who never drank any thing " but Water, fat at Table with *Pope Alexander*, " and that his Holinefs would needs tafte of his " Cup ; left his abftemioufnefs fhould be known, " God turn'd the Water into Wine : fo that the " *Pope* found nothing but Wine in the Cup. But " when *Becket* pledg'd him, it was turn'd into Wa-" ter again."

Laughing therefore, and *Ridicule* in *ferious Matters*, go round the World with no inconfiderable Applaufe, and feem highly proper for this World of Nonfenfe and Folly. To hinder *laughing* upon fuch juft Occafions as are given, is almoft all one

---

* De Divin. l. 2. c. 25.   † *Rog. Hoveden*, Pars ii. p. 520.

as

as to hinder *breathing.* A very witty, drolling, Dramatick Poet, and of the firſt Rank for Quality, ſays in a *Prologue* to his Auditors.

> " *Suppoſe now, at this Inſtant, one of you*
> " *Were tickled by a Fool, what would you do?*
> " *'Tis ten to one you'd* laugh : *here's juſt the Caſe.*
> " *For there are Fools that tickle with their Face.*
> " *Your gay Fool tickles with his Dreſs and Motions* ;
> " *But your* grave Fool *of Fools with* ſilly Notions.
> " *Is it not then unjuſt that Fops ſhould ſtill*
> " *Force one to* laugh, *and then take laughing ill?*

II. *Secondly,* If it be a Fault in thoſe reverend Divines, mention'd in the foregoing Article, to uſe *Irony, Drollery, Ridicule,* and *Satire,* in any Caſe ; or if the Fault lies in an exorbitant Uſe thereof, or in any particular Species of *Drollery* ; as, for example, ſuch *Drollery* as is to be found in the polemical Writings and Sermons of Dr. *South* ; it is fit ſome Remedy ſhould be employ'd for the Cure of this Evil. And the Remedy I would propoſe, ſhould not be to have the Authors puniſh'd by the Magiſtrate, any more than for any other Faults in writing ; but either to neglect and deſpiſe it, as Rage and Scolding, which drop into Oblivion with the Sound, and would have a Life given it by Reſentment : or to allow Men to *criticize* and *ridicule* one another for their *Ironies* and *Drollery,* and to exerciſe their Wit and Parts againſt each other ; that being the true Method to bring Things to a Standard, to fix the Decency and Propriety of Writing, to teach Men how to write to the Satisfaction of the ingenious, polite, and ſenſible Part of Mankind : for Decency and Propriety will ſtand the Teſt of Ridicule, and triumph over all the falſe Pretences to Wit ; and Indecency and Impropriety

B 3 will

will fink under the Trial of Ridicule, as being capable
of being baffled by Reason, and juftly ridicul'd.
And if any kind or degree of *Ridicule* be abfurd or
ridiculous, that will appear fo upon Trial, no lefs
than the low and grofs *Ridicule* prevalent among the
unpolite Part of the World : But that will never
appear. On the contrary, *Ridicule* of certain kinds,
and under reafonable Directions and Rules, and ufed
in proper Time, Place, and Manner, (all which
alfo are only to be found out and fix'd by Trial and
Experience) is both a proper and neceffary Method
of Difcourfe in many Cafes, and efpecially in the
Cafe of *Gravity*, when that is attended with Hypocrify or Impofture, or with Ignorance, or with
fourenefs of Temper and Perfecution : all which
ought to draw after them the *Ridicule* and *Contempt*
of the Society, which has no other effectual Remedy againft fuch Methods of Impofition. And to
determine in fome meafure the Nature and Extent
of the *Irony* I contend for, as *Juft*, I profefs to approve the noble *Sarcafm* of *Elijah* *; wherein he
thus mocks the *Priefts* of *Baal*, faying in effect to
them, " *Cry aloud*, for your *Baal* is a fine God:
" *He is either talking, or he is purfuing, or he is in a*
" *Journey; or peradventure he fleepeth, and muft be*
" *awaked*." And I concur with the *Pfalmift* †, who
thought it no Indecency to fay, that *he that fits in*
Heaven fhall laugh them (that is, certain Kings, who
were *David's* Enemies) *to fcorn ; the Lord fhall have*
them in Derifion : and muft judge, that *laughing to*
fcorn, and *deriding* the greateft Men upon Earth,
even Kings and Princes, to be a laudable and divine
Method of dealing with them, who are only to be
taught or rebuk'd in fome artful way. I alfo approve of the following *Sarcafm* or *Irony*, which

* 1 *Kings* xviii.   † *Pfalm* ii. 4.

has

has a better Authority for it than *Elijah* or the *Pſalmiſt*. *Moſes* introduces God ſpeaking thus after the Fall [*], *Behold the Man is become like one of us, to know Good and Evil!* And I think this Paſſage ſhews, that the whole Affair of the *Fall*, of which we have ſo very brief an Account, was a very entertaining Scene ; and would have appear'd ſo, if ſet forth at large ; as indeed it does under the Hands of our Divines, who have ſupplied that ſhort Narration by various Additions, founded on Conjectures, and particularly under the fine Hand of Dr. *Tho. Burnet*, who has made a moſt ingenious Dialogue of what he ſuppos'd paſs'd between *Eve* and the *Serpent* [‡]. To ſay nothing of *Milton*'s famous *Paradiſe Loſt*.

In fine, ever ſince I could read the *Bible*, I was particularly pleas'd with the *Hiſtory* of *Jonas*, where ſuch a Repreſentation is made of that *Prophet*'s Ignorance, Folly, and Peeviſhneſs, as expoſes him to the utmoſt Contempt and Scorn, and fixes a perpetual *Ridicule* on his Character. And let me here obſerve, that this *Hiſtory* has had ample Juſtice done it, in an Explication thereof by *two* [†] very ingenious Authors, who, by moſt penetrating and happy Criticiſms and Reflections, have drawn the Character of *Jonas* in a more open manner.

III. But, *Thirdly*, I wave my *Remedy*, and am ready to come into any Law that ſhall be made to rectify this ſuppos'd Fault of *Irony*, by puniſhing thoſe who are guilty of it.

The great Concern is and ought to be, that *the Liberty of examining into the Truth of Things ſhould be*

[*] *Gen.* iii. 22.
[‡] Archæolog. Philoſ. *l. 2. c. 7.*
[†] Shaftesbury *in Charact.* Vol. 3. *and* Whitchcot's *Sermons:* Vol. 1.

kept

kept up, that Men may have some Sense and Know-ledge, and not be the *Dupes* of *Cheats* and *Impostors*, or of those who would keep them in the dark, and let them receive nothing but thro' their Hands. If that be secur'd to us by Authority, I, for my part, am very ready to sacrifice the Privilege of *Irony*, tho so much in fashion among all Men ; being per-suaded, that a great Part of the *Irony* complain'd of, has its rise from the *want of Liberty to examine into the Truth of Things*; and that if that *Liberty* was prevalent, it would, without a Law, prevent all that *Irony* which Men are driven into for want of Liberty to speak plainly, and to protect them-selves from the Attacks of those who would take the Advantage to ruin them for direct Assertions ; and that such Authors as *Rabelais, Saint Aldegonde, Blount, Marvel, Hickeringil,* and many others, would never have run into that Excess of *Burlesque,* for which they are all so famous, had not the Restraint from writing *seriously* been so great.

" If * Men are forbid to speak their Minds
" *seriously* on certain Subjects, they will do it *ironi-*
" *cally.* If they are forbid at all upon such Subjects,
" or if they find it dangerous to do so, they will
" then redouble their Disguise, involve themselves
" in mysteriousness, and talk so as hardly to be un-
" derstood, or at least not plainly interpreted by
" those who are dispos'd to do them a Mischief. And
" thus *Raillery* is brought more in fashion, and
" runs into an Extreme. 'Tis the persecuting Spi-
" rit has rais'd the *bantering* one : And want of Li-
" berty may account for want of a true Politeness,
" and for the Corruption or wrong Use of Pleasan-
" try and Humour.

* Shaftesbury's *Characteristicks,* Vol. I. p. 71.

" If

" If in this refpect we ftrain the juft Meafure of
" what we call *Urbanity*, and are apt fometimes to
" take a buffooning ruftick Air, we may thank
" the ridiculous Solemnity and four Humour of
" our *Pedagogues :* or rather they may thank
" themfelves, if they in particular meet with the
" heavieft of this kind of Treatment. For it will
" naturally fall heavieft, where the Conftraint has
" been the fevereft. The greater the Weight is,
" the bitterer will be the Satire. The higher
" the Slavery, the more exquifite the Buffoonery.

" That this is really fo, may appear by looking
" on thofe Countries where the fpiritual Tyranny
" is higheft. For the greateft of *Buffoons* are the
" *Italians :* and in their Writings, in their freer
" fort of Converfations, on their Theatres, and in
" their *Streets*, *Buffoonery* and *Burlefque* are in the
" higheft Vogue. 'Tis the only manner in which
" the poor cramp'd Wretches can difcharge a free
" Thought. We muft yield to 'em the Superio-
" rity in this fort of Wit. For what wonder is it
" if we, who have more Liberty, have lefs Dex-
" terity in that egregious way of *Raillery* and
" *Ridicule ?*"

Liberty of *grave* Examination being fix'd by Law,
I am, I fay, ready to facrifice the Privilege of
Irony, and yield to have a Law enacted to prevent it. I am, moreover, willing to leave the
drawing up fuch a Law to your felf; who honeft-
ly and impartially fay*, that all who *droll*, let them
be of any Party, let them *droll for the Truth or
againft it*, fhould be equally punifh'd.

Thus this grand Affair of *Irony*, *Banter*, and
Ridicule ; this laft perfecuting Pretence, upon which
you would fet the Humours and Paffions of Peo-

* *Page* 307.

ple,

ple, who are all at quiet, on float, and make a Fermentation, and raise a Persecution against particular People, seems perfectly settled, by yielding to your own Terms.

IV. Let me here add, that I am apt to think, that when you draw up your Law, you will find it so very difficult to settle the Point of *Decency* in Writing, in respect to all the various kinds of *Irony* and *Ridicule*, that you will be ready to lay aside your Project; and that you will be no more able to settle that *Point of Decency*, than you would be to settle by Law, that *Cleanliness* in Clothes, and that Politeness in Dress, Behaviour, and Conversation, which become Men of Quality and Fortune in the World, and should be habitual to them: And that, if you are able to do that to your own Satisfaction, you will find it very difficult to engage the Lawmakers in your Project. For I am persuaded, that if our Lawmakers were, out of a rational Principle, disposed to give Liberty by Law to a *serious* Opposition to publickly receiv'd Notions, they would not think it of much Importance to make a *Law* about a Method of *Irony*. They will naturally conclude, that if Men may and ought to be allow'd to write *seriously* in Opposition to publickly receiv'd Doctrines, they should be allow'd to write in their own way; and will be unwilling to be depriv'd of ingenious and witty Discourses, or such as some of them will judge so, about a Subject wherein *serious free* Discourse is allow'd. Besides, I am apt to think, that you, upon consideration of the Advantages which the Church has receiv'd from the *Berkenheads*, the *Heylins*, the *Ryves's*, the *Needhams*, the *Lestranges*, the *Nalsons*, the *Lesleys*, the *Oldesworths*, and others, in their *Mercurius Aulicus's*, their *Mercurius Pragmaticus's*,

their

their *Mercurius Rusticus's*, their *Observators* *, their *Heraclitus Ridens's*, *Rehearsals*, their *Examiners* †, and the three Volumes against the *Rights of the Church*; from the *Butlers* in their *Hudibras's*, and other Burlesque Works upon the Religion and Religious Conduct of the Dissenters; or from the *Eachards*, the *Tom Browns*, and *Swifts*; or from the *Parkers* ‡, *Patricks* ††, *Souths* **, *Sherlocks* ‖,

Atter-

---

* *How useful Lestrange's* Observators, *which were design'd to expose the Dissenters to Contempt and Persecution, were deem'd to the Church at the time they were publish'd, may be judged of by Bp.* Burnet, *who says [in his* Eighteen Papers, p. 90.] "An-" "other Buffoon was hired to plague the Nation with three or" "four Papers a Week, which to the Reproach of the Age in" "which we live, had but too great and too general Effect, for" "poisoning the Spirits of the Clergy."*

† *In this Work the Dissenters and Low Churchmen are sufficiently rally'd and abus'd, and particularly the Free-Thinkers, whose Creed is therein represented as consisting of these two Negatives,* No Queen and no God. Examiners, *Vol.* 3. p. 12.

Mr. Addison *tells us* [Freeholder N°. 19.] "*the Examiner*" "*was the favourite Work of the Party. It was usher'd into the*" "*World by a Letter from a Secretary of State, setting forth the*" "*great Genius of the Author, the Usefulness of his Design, and*" "*the mighty Consequences that were to be expected from it. It*" "*is said to be written by those among them whom they look'd*" "*upon as their most celebrated Wits and Politicians, and was*" "*dispers'd into all Quarters of the Nation with great Industry*" "*and Expence.*——— *In this Paper all the great Men who had*" "*done eminent Services to their Country, but a few Years before,*" "*were draughted out one by one, and baited in their Turns. No*" "*Sanctity of Character, or Privilege of Sex exempted Persons.*" "——*Several of our Prelates were the standing Marks of pub-*" "*lick Raillery.*———

‡ *In his* Ecclesiastical Policy, *his* Defence *and* Continuation *thereof, and his* Reproof *to* Marvel's Rehearsal transpos'd.

†† *In his* Friendly Debates.

** *In his six Volumes of* Sermons, *and in his* Books *of the* Trinity.

‖ *In his* Discourse of the Knowledge of Christ, &c. *his* Defences *of Dr.* Stillingfleet's Unreasonableness of Separation, *and his* Answer *to the* Protestant Reconciler.

Atterburys *, and *Sacheverels* †; in their Difcourfes, and
Tracts againft the Nonconformifts, Whigs, Low-
Church-men, and Latitudinarians ; and other fuch
ironical, fatirical, and polemical Divines ; and
from fuch *drolling* Judges as *Howel, Recorder* of
London, and the Chief Juftice *Jefferys*, who, in
all Caufes, where *Whigs* or Diffenters were the
Perfons accus'd and try'd before them, carried on
the Trial by a ‖ Train of ridicule on them, their
Witneffes and Counfel : I fay, I am apt to think,
that you would be unwilling to be depriv'd of
what has been and may be again fo ferviceable.

I am difpos'd to think that Dr. *Snape*, who is
notorioufly known to have gone into the greateft
Lengths of Calumny and Satire againft Bifhop
Hoadley ‡, to have fall'n upon the diffenting Clergy
in a burlefque and bantering Addrefs to the *Peirces*,
the *Calamys*, and the *Bradburys*, and to have
written a long *ironical Letter* in the Name of the
Jefuits to Mr. *de la Pilloniere* ††, will be thought a
very improper Object of Cenfure for fuch Employ-
ment of his Pen. On the contrary, fuch fort of
Attacks upon fuch Perfons are the moft meritori-
ous Parts of a Man's Life, recommend him as a
Perfon of true and fincere Religion, much more
than the ftrongeft Reafoning, and the moft regular
Life ; and pave the way to all the Riches, and Plea-
fures,

---

* *In his Tranflation of* Dryden's Abfalom *and* Achitophel *into Latin Verfe, whereby he was firft flufh'd ; and in his* Convocational Controverfy, *and in his numerous State Libels.*

† *In his Sermons,* Rights of the Church, *and efpecially his*
Character *of a* Low-Church-man, *drawn to abufe Bifhop*
Floyd

‖ *Of this, the Trials of* Penn *and* Mead *before* Howel, *and of*
Baxter *before* Jefferys, *are, Mafter Pieces ; of which laft you
have an Account, in* Kennet's Compleat Hiftory of England,
Vol. 3d. and of the former in the Phœnix, *Vol. 1.*

‖ Snape's Vindication *againft* Pilloniere. p. 50.
†† *Id.* p. 63.

fures, and Advantages of Life; not only among thofe, who, under the Colour of Religion, are carrying on a common *Corporation Caufe* of Wealth, Power, and Authority, but among many well-meaning People, who allow of all Practices, which they fuppofe help out the *Truth!* It feems to me a moft prodigious Banter upon us, for Men to talk in general of the *Immorality* of *Ridicule* and *Irony*, and of *punifhing* Men for thofe Matters, when their own Practice is *univerfal Irony* and *Ridicule* of all thofe who go not with them, and *univerfal Applaufe* and *Encouragement* for fuch *Ridicule* and *Irony*, and diftinguifhing by all the honourable ways imaginable fuch *drolling* Authors for their Drollery; and when Punifhment for *Drollery* is never call'd for, but when *Drollery* is ufed or employ'd againft them!

I don't know whether you would be willing, if you confider of it, to limit the Stage it felf, which has with great Applaufe and Succefs, from Queen *Elizabeth*'s Time downwards, ridicul'd the ferious *Puritans* and *Diffenters*, and that without any Complaints from *good Churchmen*, that *ferious* Perfons and Things were *banter'd* and *droll'd* upon; and has triumph'd over its fanatical Adverfaries in the Perfon of *Pryn*, who fufficiently fuffer'd for his *Hiftrio-Maftix*, and has been approv'd of as an innocent Diverfion by the religious Dr. *Patrick* in his *Friendly Debate*, in the Reign of King *Charles* II. when the Stage was in a very immoral State. I don't know whether you would be willing even to reftrain *Bartholomew Fair*, where the Sect of the *New Prophets* was the Subject of a *Droll* or *Puppet-Show*, to the great Satisfaction of the Auditors, who, it may be prefum'd, were all good Churchmen, *Puritans* and *Diffenters* ufually declining fuch Entertainments out

of

of *real* or *pretended* Serioufnefs. (" A certain
" Clergyman thought fit to remark, that King
" *William* could be no good Churchman, becaufe
" of his not frequenting the *Play-Houfe*."*)

V. It will probably be a Motive with you to be
againft abolifhing *Drollery*, when you reflect that
the Men of *Irony*, the *Droles* and *Satirifts*, have been
and always will be very numerous on your fide,
where they have been and are fo much incourag'd
for acting that Part, and that they have always been
and always will be very few on the fide of *Heterodoxy*;
a Caufe wherein an Author by engaging, may
hurt his Reputation and Fortune, and can propofe
nothing to himfelf but Poverty and Difgrace. I
doubt whether you would be for punifhing your
Friend Dr. *Rogers*, from whom I juft now quoted an
Irony on the Author of *The Scheme of Literal Prophecy
confider'd*, or any one elfe, for *laughing* at and making
fport with him; or whether you would be
for punifhing the Reverend Mr. *Trapp*, who implies
the *Juftnefs* and *Propriety of ridiculing Popery*; when
he fays †, that *Popery is fo foolifh and abfurd, that
every body of common Senfe muft* L A U G H *at it* ; and
when he refers to *Erafmus* for having *abundantly*
R I D I C U L'D their *Reliques* ; and himfelf puts *Ridicule*
in Practice againft them, by reprefenting their
Doctrines and Practices as *ridiculoufly foolifh*, as *defpicably
childifh*, and *Matter of mere Scorn* ; as *monftrous*;
as *Spells, juggling Tricks, grofs Cheats, Impoftures* ‡,
and *wretched Shifts* ; and in fine, in reprefenting by
way of *Specimen*, all their *Miracles* as *Legends*; of
which he fays, *Thefe and a thoufand more fuch like
unreafonable Lies, which a Child of common Senfe*

* *The Stage condemn'd*, p. 2.
† Popery truly ftated, *p.* 127, 128.
‡ *Pag.* 75, 76, 77, 79, 81, 112, 113, 120, 122, 124,
125.

F *would*

*would laugh at, are impos'd upon and swallow'd by
the ignorant People, and make a* VERY GREAT P*art
of the Popish Religion.*

And this, in concurrence with Mr. *Trapp*, I
also take to be the Cafe of Popery, that it muft
make Men *laugh*; and that it is much eafier to be
gravely difpofed in reading a *Stage-Comedy* or *Farce*,
than in confidering and reflecting on the *Comedy* and
Farce of *Popery*; than which, Wit and Folly, and
Madnefs in conjunction, cannot invent or make a
thing more ridiculous, according to that Light in
which I fee their Doctrines, Ceremonies and Worfhip, the Hiftories and Legends of their Saints,
and the pretended Miracles wrought in their Church;
which has hardly any thing *ferious* in it but its Per-
fecutions, its Murders, its Maffacres; all employ'd
againft the moft innocent and virtuous, and the
moft fenfible and learned Men, becaufe they will
not be *Tools* to fupport Villany and Ignorance.

" Tranfubftantiation, fays *Tillotfon* *, is not a
" Controverfy of Scripture againft Scripture, or of
" Reafon againft Reafon, but of downright Impu-
" dence againft the plain meaning of Scripture,
" and all the Senfe and Reafon of Mankind."
And accordingly he fcruples not to fay, in a moft
drolling manner, that " Tranfubftantiation is one
" of the chief of the *Roman* Church's *legerdemain*
" and *juggling Tricks* of Falfhood and Impofture;
" and that in all Probability thofe common jug-
" gling Words of *Hocus-pocus*, are nothing elfe but a
" Corruption of *hoc eft corpus*, by way of ridiculous
" Imitation of the Church of *Rome* in their *Trick*
" of *Tranfubftantiation*." And as he *archly* makes
the Introduction of this monftrous Piece of *grave
Nonfenfe* to be owing to its being at firft preach'd
by its Promoters with *convenient Gravity and Solem-*

* *Sermons*, Vol. III. p. 299.

nity *, which is the common Method of impofing Abfurdities on the World ; fo I think that Doctrine taught with fuch *convenient Gravity and Solemnity* fhould neceffarily produce *Levity, Laughter and Ridicule,* in all intelligent People to whom it is propos'd, who muft *fmile,* if they can with fafety, to fee fuch Stuff vented with a grave Face.

In like manner many other Divines treat and laugh at *Popery.* Even the folemn and grave Dr. *Whitby* has written a Book againft *Tranfubftantiation,* under the Title of " Irrifio Dei Panarii, *The Derifion of the* " *Breaden God,*" in Imitation of the primitive Fathers, who have written *Derifions* and *Mockeries* of the *Pagan* Religion.

And he takes the Materials whereof this drolling Performance of his confifts, from the *holy Scriptures,* the *Apocryphal Books,* and *Writings* of the *holy Fathers,* as he tells us in his Title-Page ; three inexhauftible Sources of Wit and Irony againft the Corrupters of true and genuine Religion. In like manner he turns upon the Popifh Clergy the feveral Arguments urg'd by the *Jewifh* Clergy in the *New Teftament,* for the Authority of the *Jewifh* Church ; and anfwers, under that *Irony,* all that the Popifh Clergy offer in behalf of the *Authority* of their *Church,* in a *Sermon* at the End of his *Annotations* on St. *John's Gofpel.*

Nor do our Divines confine their *Derifions, Ridicule* and *Irony* againft *Popery* to their Treatifes and Difcourfes, but fill their *Sermons,* and efpecially their *Sermons* on the *Fifth of November,* and other political *Days,* with infinite Reflections of that Kind. Of thefe *Reflections* a Popifh Author publifh'd a *Specimen,* in a Book intitled †, *Good Advice*

---

* Rule of Faith, *p.* 347, 348.
† See *p.* 57.

to *Pulpits*, in order to shame the Church out of their Method of *drolling* and *laughing* * at *Popery*. But this Book had no other effect, than to produce a *Defence* of those *Sermons* under the Title of *Pulpit Popery true Popery*, vindicating the several *Droll* Representations made of *Popery* in those *Sermons*.

Of these *drolling* Reflections cited by the Popish Author out of our Church of *England Sermons*, take these following for a Specimen of what are to be met with in those *Sermons* †.

" Pilgrimages, going Bare-foot, Hair-shirts,
" and Whips, with other such Gospel-artillery, are
" their only Helps to Devotion.——It seems that
" with them a Man sometimes cannot be a Peni-
" tent, unless he also turns Vagabond, and foots it
" to *Jerusalem*.——He that thinks to expiate a
" Sin by going bare-foot, does the Penance of a
" Goose, and only makes one Folly the Atone-
" ment of another. *Paul* indeed was scourg'd
" and beaten by the *Jews*; but we never read that
" he beat or scourg'd himself; and if they think
" his keeping under his Body imports so much,
" they must first prove that the Body cannot be
" kept under by a virtuous Mind, and that the
" Mind cannot be made virtuous but by a Scourge ;
" and consequently, that Thongs and Whipcord
" are Means of Grace, and Things necessary to
" Salvation. The truth is, if Mens Religion lies
" no deeper than their Skin, it is possible they
" may scourge themselves into very great Im-
" provements.——But they will find that bodily
" Exercise touches not the Soul ; and consequently
" that in this whole Course they are like Men out
" of the way: let them flash on never so fast, they

" are

" are not at all nearer their Journey's-end : And
" howsoever they deceive themselves and others,
" they may as well expect to bring a Cart, as a
" Soul, to Heaven.

" What say you to the Popish Doctrine of the
" *Sacrifice of the Mass.* —— According to this
" Doctrine, our blessed Saviour must still, to the
" end of the World, be laid hold on by Sinners,
" be ground with their Teeth, and sent down into
" their impure Paunches, as often as the Priest
" shall pronounce this Charm, *hoc est corpus meum :*
" and it seems that he was a false Prophet, when
" he said upon the Cross, *It is finish'd,* seeing there
" was such an infinite deal of *loathsom Drudgery* still
" to be undergone.

" For *Purgatory,* 'tis not material in it self, whe-
" ther it be, or where it be, no more than the
" World in the Moon ; but so long as that false
" Fire serves to maintain a true one, and his Holi-
" ness's Kitchen smokes with the Rents he receives
" for releasing Souls from thence, which never
" came there, it concerns him and his to see to it,
" that it be not suffer'd to go out."

An ingenious Author, Sir *Richard Steel,* has of
late made a *Dedication* to his *Holiness* the *Pope* himself, before a Book entitled, *An Account of the
State of the Roman Catholick Religion throughout the
World,* &c. In which *Dedication,* that most exalted
Clergyman the *Pope,* that [suppos'd] infallible Dic-
tator in Religion, and most grave Person ; who, if
serious Matters and Persons were always to be treated *seriously,* may vie with any other Mortal for a
Right to *serious* Treatment ; is expos'd by incomparable *Drollery* and *Irony* to the utmost Contempt, to
the universal Satisfaction of Protestant Readers, who
have been pleas'd to see a gross Impostor, however
respected

respected and ador'd by godly and serious Papists, so treated.

VI. In fine, it is suited to the common Practice of this Nation to ridicule *Popery*, as well as *Nonconformity* ; and tho several *grave* Books, written among us against Popery, in the Reign of King *James* II. (of which yet the *Romish* Priests complain'd, as treating the King's * *Religion* with Contempt) were then very well receiv'd and applauded for Learning and strength of Arguing ; yet, I believe, it may with more Propriety be said, that King *James* II. and *Popery* were † *laugh'd* or *Lilli-bullero'd*, than that they were *argu'd* out of the Kingdom.

The reading the *King's Declaration of Indulgence* in Churches 1688, had this fatal *Jest* put upon it by a reverend Divine, " Who pleasantly told his " People, *That tho he was obliged to read it, they* " *were not obliged to hear it* ‖ ; and he stop'd till they " all went out, and then he read it to the Walls." To which may be added, the famous Mr. *Wallop*'s excellent Comparison of that *Declaration* upon the Instant of its Publication, to *the scaffolding of St. Paul's Church ; which, as soon as the Building was finish'd, would be pull'd down.*

Bishop *Burnet* celebrates, with the greatest Justness, our Taste, and indeed the Taste of the World in this Respect, when he relates how *Popery* was then used among us ; and he recites some of the *Jests* which passed and were received with universal Applause. He tells us ††, " The Court was now (that is, in " 1686,) much set on making Converts, which " fail'd in most Instances, and produc'd *Repartees* ; " that whether true or false, were much repeated,

* Burnet's History of his own Times, *p.* 674.
† Ib. *p.* 792. ‖ Ibid. *p.* 740. †† Ibid. *p.* 683.

C 2

" and

" and were heard with great Satisfaction. The
" Earl of *Mulgrave* (since Duke of *Buckinghamshire*)
" was Lord Chamberlain ; he was apt to comply
" in every thing that he thought might be ac-
" ceptable, for he went with the King to Mass,
" and kneeled at it ; and being look'd on as indif-
" ferent to all Religions, the Priests made an At-
" tack upon him : He heard them *gravely* arguing
" for *Transubstantiation*. He told them he was wil-
" ling to receive Instruction ; he had taken much
" Pains to bring himself to believe in God, who
" made the World and all Men in it : But it must
" not be an ordinary Force of Argument that could
" make him believe that Man was quits with God,
" and made God again. The Earl of *Middleton*
" had marry'd into a Popish Family, and was a
" Man of great Parts and a generous Temper, but
" of loose Principles in Religion ; so a Priest was
" sent to instruct him. He began with *Transub-*
" *stantiation*, of which he said he would convince
" him immediately : And began thus, You be-
" lieve the *Trinity*. *Middleton* stop'd him, and
" said, who told you so ? At which he seem'd a-
" mazed. So the Earl said, he expected he should
" convince him of his Belief, but not question him
" of his own : With this the Priest was so disor-
" der'd, that he could proceed no farther. One
" Day the King gave the Duke of *Norfolk* the
" Sword of State to carry before him to the Chap-
" pel, and he stood at the Door. Upon which the
" King said to him, My Lord, your Father would
" have gone farther. To which the Duke answer'd,
" Your Majesty's Father was the better Man, and
" he would not have gone so far. *Kirk* was also
" spoken to, to change his Religion, and he reply'd
" briskly, that he was already pre-engag'd, for *he*
" *had promis'd the King of* Morocco, *that if ever*
" *he*

" *he chang'd his Religion he would turn* Mahometan."
When K. *James* sent an *Irish* Priest to convert the D. of
Bucks [*Villers*] the said Duke entertain'd the Priest with
a Bottle, and engag'd him in a *Dialogue*, which the
Duke afterwards caus'd to be printed, to the no
small Mortification of all Papists, who were therein
exceedingly ridicul'd, and to the Triumph of all
good Churchmen, who are never better pleas'd,
than when they have the *Laugh* on their side.

At this time also were publish'd two merry Books,
by a couple of our Divines, with express View to
make Protestants laugh at *Popery*, as at a *Farce* ;
and they were, *The School of the Eucharist*, wherein
is a Collection of ridiculous *Miracles*, pretended to
be wrought to support the Truth of *Transubstantiation*, and *Purgatory prov'd by Miracles*.

I must not omit another incomparable Piece of
Wit and Raillery against *Popery*, publish'd at that
time. It seems the famous Poet, *Dryden*, thought
fit to declare himself a *Roman Catholick* ; and had,
as 'tis said, a *Penance* injoyn'd him by his Confessor,
for having formerly written *The Spanish Fryar*, of
composing some *Treatise* in a *poetical way* for *Popery*,
and against the *Reformation*. This he executed in a
Poem, intituled, *The Hind and Panther* ; which, setting aside the Absurdity of the Matters therein af-
serted, and of the several Arguments to maintain
them, is, in other Respects, one of the most mean
Compositions that ever the Press produc'd. Was
it proper to pass over in silence such a Work, from
whence probably the Popish Party expected great
Matters, as knowing the Efficacy of Poetry, and
being Witnesses of the Success the Author had had
in his *Absalom* and *Achitophel* against the *Whigs* ?
Was it proper to write *seriously* and *gravely* against
a Book, wherein the Author every where aims at
Wit, Irony, and Burlesque, and does himself make

ſo ridiculous a Figure, as to be a ſtanding Jeſt throughout the whole ? Was not the Convert himſelf, as ſuch, a *Jeſt*, or as profeſſing any Religion, a-*Jeſt*; who argu'd for Pay, and ſpoke as he was brib'd, and would have profeſs'd any Opinions, as is the Mode and Practice of the World, to which Salary and Preferments are annexed ? Some ingenious Perſons of the Times took a better Method, and agreeably to the Temper and Diſpoſition of our Countrymen, and to the nature of *Dryden's* Attack, and his intereſted Writing for Religion, made a Return in a Paper intituled, *The Hind and Panther tranſvers'd to the Story of the Country-Mouſe and City-Mouſe :* Out of which, for a Specimen of *juſt Irony*, and *fine Raillery*, I will give you the following Paſſage.

" *Sirrah,* ſays Brindle, *thou haſt brought us Wine,*
" *Sour to my Taſte, and to my Eyes unfine.*
" Says Will, *All Gentlemen like it. Ah !* ſays White,
" *What is approv'd by them muſt needs be right.*
" *'Tis true, I thought it bad, but if the* Houſe
" *Commend it, I ſubmit,* a private Mouſe.
" *Nor to their Catholick Conſent oppoſe*
" *My erring Judgment and reforming Noſe.*
" * *Why, what a Devil, ſhan't I truſt my Eyes,*
" *Muſt I drink Stum, becauſe the Raſcal lies,*
" *And palms upon us* Catholick *Conſent,*
" *To give* ſophiſticated Brewings *Vent ?*
" Says White, *what antient Evidence can ſway,*
" *If you muſt argue thus and not obey ?*
" Drawers *muſt be truſted, thro' whoſe hands con-*
" *You take the Liquor, or you ſpoil the Trade.* (vey'd
" *For ſure thoſe* honeſt Fellows *have no Knack*
" *Of putting off ſtum'd Claret for* Pontack.

* *The Proteſtant Mouſe ſpeaks.*

" *How*

" *How long alas! would the poor Vintner laft,*
" *If all that drink muft* judge, *and every Gueft* }
" *Be allow'd to have an underftanding* Tafte ?

VII. I queftion whether High-Church would be
willing to have the reverend Author of the *Tale of
a Tub*, one of the greateft *Droles* that ever appear'd upon the Stage of the World, punifh'd for
that or any other of his *drolling* Works: For tho.
religious Matters, and all the various Forms of
Chriftianity have therein a confiderable Share of *Ridicule*; yet in regard of his *Drollery* upon the *Whigs,
Diffenters,* and the *War* with *France* (things of as
ferious and weighty Confideration, and as much af-·
fecting the Peace of Society, as *Juftification* by *Faith*·
only, Predeftination, Tranfubftantiation, or *Conftan-
fubftantiation,* or *Queftions* about *religious Ceremonies,*
or any fuch interefted Matters) the *Convocation*
in their famous *Reprefentation* of the *Profanenefs* and
Blafphemy of the Nation, took no notice of his
drolling on Chriftianity : And his Ufefulnefs in *Drollery* and *Ridicule* was deem'd fufficient by the *Pious*
Queen *Anne,* and her *pious Miniftry,* to intitle him to
a Church Preferment of feveral hundred Pounds
per Ann. * which fhe beftow'd upon him, notwith-·
ftanding a *fanatick High-Churchman,* who weakly
thought *Serioufnefs* in Religion of more ufe toHigh-
Church than *Drollery,* and attempted to hinder his
Promotion, by reprefenting to her Majefty, " What
" a Scandal it would be both to Church and State
" to beftow Preferment upon a Clergyman, who
" was hardly fufpected of being a Chriftian."
Befides, High-Church receives daily moft fignal
Services from his drolling Capacity, which has of
late exerted itfelf on the Jacobite Stage of *Mift's*

* **Boyer's** Life of Queen *Anne,* in the Annual Lift of the
Deaths, *p.* 65.

and

and *Fogg's* Journal, and in other little Papers publifh'd in *Ireland*; in which he endeavours to expofe
the prefent Adminiftration of publick Affairs to
contempt, to inflame the *Irifh* Nation againft the
Englifh, and to make them throw off all Subjection
to the *Englifh* Government, to fatirize Bifhop *Burnet* and other *Whig* Bifhops; and, in fine, to pave the
way for a new or Popifh Revolution, as far as
choofing the moft proper Topicks of Invective,
and treating of them in the way of *Drollery*, can do.

VIII. It is well known, that Gravity, Precifenefs,
Solemnity, Sournefs, formal Drefs and Behaviour,
Sobriety of Manners, keeping at a diftance from
the common Paftimes of the World, Averfion to
Rites and Ceremonies in the publick Worfhip, and
to Pictures, Images, and Mufick in Churches;
mixing Religion in common Converfation, ufing
long Graces, practifing Family-Worfhip, part of
which was praying *ex tempore*; fetting up and hearing Lectures, and a ftrict Obfervation of the Lord's-
Day, which was call'd the *Sabbath*, were the Parts
of the Character of a *Puritan*; who, it is to be obferv'd, ufually had the Imputation of Hypocrify
for his great and extraordinary Pretences to Religion: He was alfo a great Oppofer of the Court-
Meafures in the Reign of King *James* and King
Charles I. and moft zealous for Law, Liberty,
and Property, when thofe two Princes fet up for
raifing Money by their own Authority, and in con-
fequence thereof, fell into numerous other Acts of
Violence and Injuftice. It is alfo well known, that
to quell thefe Puritans, and leffen their Credit, and
baffle all their Pretences, Gaiety, Mirth, Paftimes
or Sports, were incourag'd and requir'd on Sundays of the People; that Churches were render'd

gay,

gay, theatrical, and pleafant by the Decorations,
Paintings, Mufick, and Ceremonies therein perform'd* ; and that the utmoft Ridicule was employ'd
againft fome of them, as *Enthufiafts*, and againft o-
thers of them as *Hypocrites*, and againft them
all as factious and feditious, by their Adverfaries ;
who were under no Reftraints, but incourag'd to
write with Scorn, Contempt, Raillery and Satire
againft thefe fuppos'd Enemies of Church and State.
Nor did the great Succefs of the *Puritans* in the
Field of Battle fupprefs that *Vein* and *Humour* of
Ridicule begun againft them ; but the *Laudean*
Party ftill carry'd on a Paper War with innumera-
ble Pamphlets, which all tended more or lefs to
make the World *laugh* at and *ridicule* the *Puritans*.
And I am verily perfuaded, that no Hiftory of any
other Country in the World can produce a Parallel, wherein the Principle and Practice of *Ridicule*
were ever fo ftrongly encourag'd, and fo conftantly
purfu'd, fix'd and rooted in the Minds of Men, as
it was and is in Churchmen againft Puritans and
Diffenters. Even at this Day the *Ridicule* is fo
ftrong againft the prefent Diffenters, fo promoted
by Clergy and Laity, efpecially in Villages and
fmall Country Towns, that they are unable to
withftand its Force, but daily come over in Numbers to the Church to avoid being *laugh'd* at. It
feems to me a Mark of Diftinction more likely
to laft in the Church than any other Matter that I
can obferve. Paffive Obedience, the divine Right
of Kings, *&c.* rife and fall according to particular

* *A* Clergyman *preach'd thus to his* Auditory : " *You have*
" Mofes *and* Aaron *before you, and the Organs behind you,*
" *fo are a happy People ; for what greater Comfort would mor-*
" *tal Men have ?*" See *Walker's* Sufferings, *&c.* p. 178.

Occa-

Occasions ; but *Laughter* at *Dissenters* seems fixt for ever, if they should chance to last so long.

South's Sermons, which now amount to *six Volumes*, make Reading *Jests* and *Banter* upon *Dissenters*, the religious Exercise of good Churchmen upon *Sundays*, who now can serve God (as many think they do by hearing or reading Sermons) and be as merry as at the Play-house. And *Hudibras*, which is a daily High-Church Entertainment, and a Pocket and Travelling High-Church Companion, must necessarily have a very considerable Effect, and cannot fail forming in Men that Humour and Vein of *Ridicule* upon *Dissenters* which runs thro' that Work. In a word, High-Church has constantly been an Enemy to, and a Ridiculer of the *Seriousness* of *Puritans* and *Dissenters*, whom they have ever charg'd with *Hypocrisy* for their *Seriousness*.

" After * the Civil War had broke out in 1641,
" and the King and Court had settled at *Oxford*,
" one *Birkenhead*, who had liv'd in *Laud*'s Family,
" and been made Fellow of *All Souls College* by
" *Laud*'s Means, was appointed to write a Weekly
" Paper under the Title of *Mercurius Aulicus* ; the
" first whereof was publish'd in 1642. In the Ab-
" sence of the Author, *Birkenhead*, from *Oxford*,
" it was continued by *Heylin*. *Birkenhead* pleas'd
" the Generality of Readers with his *Waggeries*
" and *Buffooneries* ; and the Royal Party were so
" taken with it, that the Author was recommend-
" ed to be Reader of *Moral Philosophy* by his Ma-
" jesty ;" who, together with the religious Electors, it is justly to be presum'd, thought *Waggery* and *Buffoonery*, not only Political, but *Religious* and *Moral*, when employ'd against *Puritans* and *Dissenters*.

* See the *Article* Heylin, in *Wood*'s Athenæ Oxon.

IX. King

IX. King *Charles* the Second's Reſtoration brought along with it glorious *High-Church* Times ; which were diſtinguiſh'd as much by *laughing* at *Diſſenters*, as by perſecuting them ; which paſs for a Pattern how Diſſenters are to be treated ; and which will never be given up, by *High-Church-men*, as faulty, for ridiculing Diſſenters.

The King himſelf, who had very good natural Parts, and a Diſpoſition to banter and ridicule e-very Body, and eſpecially the *Preſbyterians*, whoſe Diſcipline he had felt for his Lewdneſs and Irreli-gion in *Scotland*, had in his *Exile* an Education, and liv'd, among ſome of the greateſt *Droles* and *Wits* that any Age ever produc'd ; who could not but form him in that way, who was ſo well fitted by Temper for it. The Duke of *Buckingham* was his conſtant Companion. And he had a * *great Live-lineſs of Wit*, *and a peculiar Faculty of turning all things into ridicule*. He was Author of the *Re-hearſal*; which, as a moſt noble Author ſays, is† *a juſtly admir'd Piece of comick Wit*, *and has furniſh'd our beſt Wits in all their Controverſies*, *even in Religi-on and Politicks*, *as well as in the Affairs of Wit and Learning*, *with the moſt effectual and entertaining Method of expoſing Folly, Pedantry, falſe Reaſon, and ill Writing*. The Duke of *Buckingham* ‖ brought *Hobbes* to him to be his *Tutor*, who was a *Philoſo-phical Drole*, and had a great deal of *Wit* of the drolling kind. *Sheldon*, who was afterwards Arch-biſhop of *Canterbury*, and attended the King con-ſtantly in his Exile as his *Chaplain*, was an eminent *Drole*, as appears from Biſhop *Burnet*, who ſays ‡,

---

* Burnet's *Hiſt.* p. 100.
† *Characteriſticks*, Vol. I. p. 259.
‖ Burnet. *ibid.* ‡ Page 172.

that

that *he had a great Pleafantnefs of Converfation, perhaps too great.*

And *Hide*, afterwards Earl of *Clarendon*, who attended the King in his Exile, feems alfo to have been a great Drole, by Bifhop *Burnet*'s reprefenting him, as one, that *had too much Levity in his Wit, and that did not obferve the Decorum of his Poft* [*]. In a *Speech* to the Lords and Commons, *Hide* attack'd the Gravity of the Puritans, faying [†], " Very " merry Men have been very godly Men ; and if " a good Confcience be a continued Feaft, there is " no reafon but Men may be very merry at it." And upon Mr. *Baxter* and other Prefbyterian Minifters waiting on him in relation to the *Savoy Conference*, he faid to Mr. *Baxter* on the firft Salute [‡], that if " he were but as fat as Dr. *Manton*, we fhould " all do well."

No wonder therefore, that *Ridicule*, and *Raillery*, and *Satire*, fhould prevail at Court after the *Reftoration* ; and that King *Charles* the Second, who was a Wit himfelf, and early taught to laugh at his *Father's Stiffnefs* ‖, fhould be fo great a Mafter of them, and bring them into play among his Subjects ; and that he who had the moft fovereign Contempt for all Mankind, and in particular for the People and Church of *England*, fhould ufe his Talent againft them ; and that his People in return fhould give him like for like.

It is well known how he banter'd the Prefbyterian Minifters, who out of Intereft came over to him at *Breda* ; where they were placed in a Room next to his Majefty, and order'd to attend till his Majefty had done his Devotions ; who, it feems, pray'd fo artfully, and poured out fo many of

[*] Burnet *p* 95.
[†] Kennet's *Regifter*, p. 258.   [‡] *Ibid.* p. 515.
[‖] Burnet's *Hift.*

their Phrafes, which he had learned when he was in *Scotland*, where he was forced to be prefent at religious Exercifes of fix or feven Hours a-day; and had practis'd among the *Huguenot* Minifters in *France* *, who reported him to have a *fanctify'd Heart*, and to *fpeak the very Language of* Canaan. This *Ridicule* he *cover'd* with *Serioufnefs* ; having at that time Occafion for thofe Minifters, who were then his great Inftruments in reconciling the Nation to his *Reftoration*. When he had no farther Occafion for them, he was open in his *Ridicule*, and would fay, that † *Prefbyterianifm was not a Religion for a Gentleman*.

X. Would you, who are a Man of Senfe and Learning, and of fome Moderation, be for punifhing the Author of *The Difficulties and Difcouragements which attend the Study of the Scriptures in the way of private Judgment*, &c. who is fuppos'd to be a Prelate of the Church, for that Book, which is wholly an *Irony* about the moft facred Perfons and Things? Muft not the fine *Irony* it felf, and the Execution of it, with fo much Learning, Senfe, and Wit, raife in you the higheft Efteem and Admiration of the Author, inftead of a Difpofition to punifh him? Would you appear to the intelligent Part of the World fuch an Enemy to Knowledge, and fuch a Friend to the Kingdom of Darknefs, as fuch Punifhment would imply? In fine, can you fee and direct us to a better way, to make us inquire after and underftand Matters of Religion, to make us get and keep a good temper of Mind, and to plant and cultivate in us the Virtues neceffary to good Order and Peace in Society, and to eradicate

* Kennet's *Regifter*, p. 111.
† Burnet's *Hiftory*, p. 107.

the

the Vices that every where give Society so much
Disturbance, than what is prescrib'd or imply'd in
that Book? And can you think of a better *Form* of
Conveyance, or *Vehicle* for Matters of such universal
Concern to all intelligent People (if you consider
the State of the World, and the infinite Variety of
Understandings, Interests, and Designs of Men,
who are all to be address'd to at the same Time)than
his Method of *Irony?* And has not Success justify'd
his Method? For the Book has had a free Vent in
several Impressions ; has been very generally read
and applauded; has convinced Numbers, and has
been no Occasion of trouble either to Bookseller or
Author. It has also had the Advantage to have a
most ingenious *Letter* of *John Hales* of *Eton* join'd
to some Editions of it ; who by this *Letter*, as well
as by several others of his Pieces, shews himself to
have been another *Socrates,* one of the greatest
Masters of *true Wit* and *just Irony,* as well as
Learning, which the World ever produc'd; and
shews he could have writ such a Book as the *Difficulties,* &c. But if you are capable of coming into
any Measures for punishing the Author of the *Difficulties,* &c. for his *Irony,* I conceive, that you
may possibly hesitate a little in relation to the same
Author, about his *New Defence of the Bishop of* Bangor's *Sermon of the Kingdom of Christ, consider'd as
it is the Performance of a Man of Letters* ; which,
tho far below *The Difficulties,* &c. is an ingenious
Irony on that *Sermon.* You may probably, like
many others of the Clergy, approve of Satire so
well employ'd, as against that Bishop, who has suc-
ceeded Bishop *Burnet* in being the Subject of *Clergy-
Ridicule,* as well as in his Bishoprick. The Bishop
himself was very justly patient, under all Attacks
by the Reverend *Trapp, Earbery, Snape, Law,*
and *Luke Milbourne,* in his *Tom of Bedlam's Answer*

to his *Brother* Ben Hoadley, *St.* Peter's Poor *Parson
near the Exchange of Principles* ; fome of which
were of a very abufive kind, and fuch as can hardly
be parallel'd ; and did not call upon the Magiftrate
to come to his Aid againft that Author, or againft
any others of the Clergy who had attack'd him
with as great Mockery, Ridicule, and Irony, as e-
ver Bifhop had been by the profefs'd Adverfaries of
the Order ; or as ever the Bifhops had been by the
Puritans and *Libellers* in the Reigns of Queen
Elizabeth, King *James* and King *Charles* the Firft ;
or as *Lefley, Hickes, Hill, Atterbury, Binks,* and o-
ther High-Church Clergy, did the late Bifhop
Burnet. Inftead of that he took the true and proper Method, by publifhing an *Anfwer* to the faid
Irony, compos'd in the fame *ironical Strain,* intitled,
The Dean of Worcefter *ftill the fame : Or his new
Defence of the Bifhop of* Bangor's *Sermon, confider'd,
as it is the Performance of a great Critick, a Man of
Senfe, and a Man of Probity.* Which Anfwer does,
in my Opinion, as much Honour to the Bifhop,
by its Excellency in the *ironical Way,* as it does by
allowing the Method it felf, and going into that
Method, in imitation of his Reverend Brethren of
the Clergy, who appear to be under no Reftraints
from the *Immorality* or *Indecency* of treating the
Bifhop in the way of Ridicule and with the utmoft
Contempt ; but, on the contrary, to be fpurr'd on
by the *Excellency* and *Propriety* thereof to ufe it
againft him, even in the * *Pulpit,* as Part of the
religious Exercife on the *Lord's-day.*

XI. There is an univerfal Love and Practice of
Drollery and *Ridicule* in all, even the moft *ferious*

---

* *See the Bp. of* Bangor's *Preface to the* Anfwer *to the* Reprefentation *of the Lower Houfe of Convocation.*

3   Men,

Men, in the moſt *ſerious Places*, and on the moſt *ſerious Occaſions*. Go into the Privy-Councils of Princes, into Senates, into Courts of Judicature, and into the Aſſemblies of the Kirk or Church ; and you will find that Wit, good Humour, Ridicule, and Drollery, mix themſelves in all the Queſtions before thoſe Bodies ; and that the moſt ſolemn and ſour Perſon there preſent, will ever be found endeavouring, at leaſt, to crack his Jeſt, in order to raiſe a Character for Wit ; which has ſo great an Applauſe attending it, and renders Men ſo univerſally acceptable for their Converſation, and places them above the greateſt Proficients in the Sciences, that almoſt every one is intoxicated with the Paſſion of aiming at it.

In the Reports made to us of the Debates in the Houſes of Lords, Commons, and Convocation, the ſerious Parts of the Speeches there made die for the moſt part with the Sound ; but the Wit, the Irony, the Drollery, the Ridicule, the Satire, and Repartees, are thought worthy to be remember'd and repeated in Converſation, and make a Part of the Hiſtory of the Proceedings of thoſe Bodies, no leſs than their grave Tranſactions, as ſome ſuch muſt neceſſarily be.

Whoever will look into Antiquity for an Account of the Lives, Actions, and Works of the old Philoſophers, will find little remaining of them ; but ſome of their witty, drolling, and bantering Sayings, which alone have been thought worthy to be preſerv'd to Poſterity. And if you will look into the Lives of the modern Stateſmen, Philoſophers, Divines, Lawyers, &c. you will find that their witty Sayings ever make a conſiderable Part : by reporting which great Honour is intended to be done to their Memory. The great and moſt religious Philoſopher Dr. *H More*, has a great many Pieces

of

of Wit attributed to him in his *Life* by Mr. *Ward* ; who reprefents him from his Companions, ** *as one of the merriest Greeks they were acquainted with,* and tells us, that the Doctor faid in his *laft Illnefs*, to him ††, *that the merry way was that which he faw mightily to take* ; *and fo he ufed it the more.*

The great and famous Sir *Thomas More*, Lord Chancellor of *England* in *Henry* the Eighth's time, was an inexhauftible Source of *Drollery**, as his voluminous Works, which confift for the moft part of controverfial Divinity in behalf of Popery, fhow, and which are many of them written in Dialogue, the better to introduce the *drolling* Way of Writing, which he has us'd in fuch Perfection, that it is faid † *none can ever be weary of reading them, tho they be never fo long.* Nor could Death it felf, in immediate view before his Eyes, fupprefs his *merry* Humour, and hinder him from cracking *Jefts* on the *Scaffold* ; tho he was a Man of great *Piety* and *Devotion*, whereof all the World was convinced by his Conduct both in his Life and at his Death.

It is faid (as I have before obferv'd) of my Lord Chancellor *Clarendon*, that " he had too much *Levity* in his *Wit* ‡, and that he did not always ob-" ferve the *Decorum* of his Poft." Which implies not only his Approbation of *Drollery* in the moft *grave* Bufinefs, but alfo his great Knowledge of Mankind, by applying to them in that *Way*; which he knew from Experience, and efpecially from the common *drolling* ‖ Converfation in the Court of King *Charles* the Second, would recommend him to the World much more than an *impartial Adminiftration of Juftice* ; which is lefs felt, lefs underftood,

---

** *Ward's Life of Dr.* Henry More, *p.* 120. †† Ibid. *p.*122.
* *See the feveral Lives of him.*
† *Life lately printed,* 1726. P. 99,
‡ Burnet's *Hift.* p. 95.
‖ Temple's *Works,* Vol. II. p. 40.

and

and lefs taken notice of and applauded, than a *Piece of Wit*; which is generally fuppos'd to imply in it a great deal of Knowledge, and a Capacity fit for any thing.

Mr. *Whifton**, a famous Perfon among us, fets up for great *Gravity*, and propofes a Scheme of *Gravity* for the Direction of thofe who write about Religion : He is for allowing *Unbelievers*, nay for having them " invited by Authority to produce " all the real or original Evidence they think they " have difcover'd againft any Parts of the *Bible*; " againft any Parts of the *Jewifh* and *Chriftian* " Religions, in order to their being fully weigh'd " and confider'd by all learned Men ; provided at " the fame time, that the whole be done *gravely*, " and *ferioufly*, without all *Levity, Banter*, and *Ridicule*." And yet this Man, having a handle given him by Bifhop *Robinfon*'s Letter to the *Clergy* of his *Diocefs* about *New Doxologies borrow'd from Old Hereticks*, takes the advantage of the Bifhop's (fuppofed) Ignorance, Dulnefs, Stupidity, and Contradiction to himfelf, and writes and prints, like a *Tom Brown* or *Swift*, a moft *bantering* and *drolling* Letter, under the fneering Title of a *Letter of Thanks to the Right Reverend the Lord Bifhop* of London, *for his late Letter*, &c. whom, one would think, he fhould not only have fpar'd, but have applauded for his *profound Gravity*, and carrying on the Caufe of Religion in a very remarkable manner, with the moft *confummate Solemnity*. But fo ftrong was the Temptation, fo naturally productive of Mirth was the Bifhop's *Caufe*, and his *grave* Management thereof, as that he could not help laughing at the Bifhop, by himfelf ; and fo was led on mechanically to write in that Humour, and to publifh what he wrote, and

* *Collection of authentick Records*, Vol. II. p. 1099.

afterwards to defend his drole *Manner* * of attacking the Bifhop, againft thofe who took *offence* at that *Manner* of writing.

XII. The burning Papifts themfelves are not always *ferious* with us : They treat the Church and its Defenders as *fanatical*, and *laugh* at them as *fuch*, juft as the Church does the Diffenters, and have their elaborate Works of *Drollery* againft their Adverfaries. They publifh'd a Poem againft the *Reformation*, juft before the Death of Queen *Anne*, which was defign'd to have given fuch a Stroke to the Proteftant Religion among us, under the new projected Revolution, as *Hudibras* did to *Puritanifm* after the *Reftoration*. The Popifh Editor, in the Preface to the faid Poem, fays, " that the Motive of the Author " (*Thomas Ward*) for publifhing the *Hiftory of the* " *Reformation* in a *Burlefque Style* (tho a Hiftory full " of melancholy Incidents, which have diftracted " the Nation, even beyond the hope of recovery, " after fo much Blood drawn from all its Veins, " and from its Head) was that which he met with " in Sir *Roger L'Eftrange*'s Preface to the fecond " Part of his *Cit* and *Bumkin*, exprefs'd in thefe " Words ; *Tho this way of fooling is not my Talent,* " *nor Inclination ; yet I have great Authorities for* " *the taking up this Humour, in regard not only of* " *the Subject, but of the Age we live in ; which is* " *fo much upon the Drole, that hardly any thing elfe* " *will down with it.*"

And the ingenious Proteftant Editor of this Poem at *London*, which he allows to have fome Wit in it, concludes the Remarks he makes upon it, by faying, " One thing more we can't forbear " hinting at, that a Retaliation would be as happy

* *Second Letter to the Bifhop of* London, p. 3, 4.

" a

" a Thought as could enter into the Head of a Man
" of Genius and Spirit. What a fruitful Harveſt
" would the Legends, Tricks, ſpiritual Jugglings,
" Convents, and Nunneries, yield to a good Poet?
" *Buchanan* in his *Franciſcani*, and *Oldham* in his
" *Satires* on the Jeſuits, have open'd the Way,
" and we heartily wiſh ſome equal Pen would
" write the whole Myſtery of Iniquity at length."

XIII. All the old Puritan Preachers, who were
originally Divines of the Church of *England*, ſprink-
led and ſeaſon'd their Sermons with a great many
drolling Sayings againſt *Libertiniſm* and *Vice*, and a-
gainſt Church Ceremonies ; many of which Sayings
are reported and handed down to us in Books and
Converſation, as are alſo the Effects of thoſe Sayings, which we are told converted many to *Chriſt*
on the Spot, or in the Inſtant of Delivery. Nor is
that manner wholly laid aſide, but has continued to
be kept alive by ſome Hands at all times ; who
have been greatly follow'd for their Succeſs in drolling upon *Sinners*, and treating of Religion in hu-
mourſom and fantaſtical Phraſes, and fixing that
way of Religion in ſome Mens Minds.
I do not remember to have met with a more
complete Drole in the Church of *England*, or in any
other of the *laughing* or *ridiculing* Sects, than *Andrew
Marvel* of the grave *Puritan* Sect, in many Works
of his both in Proſe and Verſe, but eſpecially in his
Rehearſal Tranſproſed ; which tho writ againſt
Parker, who with great Eloquence, Learning, and
a Torrent of Drollery and Satire, had defended the
Court and Church's Cauſe, in aſſerting the Neceſſity
of Penal Laws againſt the Nonconformiſts, " was
" read from the *King* down to the Tradeſman with
" great pleaſure, on account of that Burleſque
" Strain and lively Drollery that ran thro' it,"

as

as Bishop *Burnet* tells us *. Nor were the gravest *Puritans* and Diffenters among us lefs taken and pleas'd with his Writings for their *Drollery*, than our *drole King*; tho there are fome Paffages in them, which fhould give juft Offence to chafte Ears.

I find alfo, that the *Puritans* and *Diffenters* have always born with, and allow'd of, a great Mixture of *Drollery* in their Sermons, that one would think fhould offend their Gravity, and pious Ears; and that they applaud their Minifters for fuch their Difcourfes, as much as the Church does Dr. *South* for the Ribaldry fprinkled thro'out his Sermons about the moft high Points in Divinity. They have always had fome eminent Divines among them who have been remarkable for fuch Paffages and Reflections: And thefe have never leffen'd their number of Auditors, nor drawn upon themfelves the Character of *Irreligious*; but have had the largeft Auditories of contributing Hearers, as well as of Churchmen, who came to fmile, and have been efteem'd very *pious* Men.

In fine, the *Puritans* and *Diffenters* have, like the Church, their Tafte of Humour, Irony, and Ridicule, which they promote with great Zeal, as a Means to ferve Religion: And I remember, that, among other things faid in behalf of *Bunyan*'s *Pilgrim's Progrefs*, upon the reprinting it lately by Subfcription, it was affirm'd, and that, in my Opinion, truly, " that it had infinitely out-done *The* " *Tale of a Tub*; which perhaps had not made one " Convert to Infidelity, whereas the *Pilgrim's Pro-* " *grefs* had converted many Sinners to *Chrift*."

XIV. The *Quakers* are certainly the moft *ferious* and folemn People among us in Matters of Religi-

on, and out-go the Diffenters of all other Kinds
therein : But yet the Church has no regard to them
on that Account, but takes Advantage from thence
to *ridicule* them the more, and to call their Sincerity more in queftion. And I much doubt whether
there was ever a Book written againft them by the
Divines of any Sect with perfect Decency, and that
had not its extravagant Flouts, Scorn, Banter, and
Irony, and that not only of the *laughing*, but of
the *cruel* kind : Wherein they copy'd after the *Jews*
of old, who while they profecuted *Chrift* to Death,
and carried on their High-Church Tragedy againft
him, acted againft him the *comick Scenes* * " of
" fpitting in his Face, and buffeting him with the
" Palms of their Hands, faying, *Prophefy unto us*,
" *thou Chrift, who is he that fmote thee* ;" and who,
when they had nail'd him to the Crofs, *revil'd* him
with divers *Taunts*, in which the *Chief Priefts,
Scribes, Elders*, and even the *Thieves, which were
crucified with him*, concurr'd. But yet for all this,
thefe folemn Quakers themfelves are not altogether
averfe to *Irony* and *Ridicule*, and ufe it when they
can. Their Books abound in Stories to ridicule in
their Turn the Priefts, their great and bitter Adverfaries : And they pleafe themfelves with throwing
at the Priefts the *Centuries of fcandalous Minifters*,
and the Books of the *Cobler of* Glocefter. They
have alfo their Satirift and Banterer, *Samuel Fifher*;
whofe Works, tho all wrote in the *drolling* Style and
Manner, they pride themfelves in, and have collected
into one great Volume in *Folio* ; in which Quaker-
Wit and Irony are fet up againft Church, Prefbyterian, and Independent Wit and Irony, without the
leaft Scruple of the lawfulnefs of fuch Arms. In a
word, their Author acts the Part of a *Jack-Pudding*,

* *Mat.* xxvi. 67, 68.

Merry

Merry Andrew, or *Buffoon*, with all the feeming
Right, Authority, and Privilege, of the Member
of fome Eftablifh'd Church of abufing all the
World but themfelves. The *Quakers* have alfo
encourag'd and publifh'd a moft arch Book of the
famous *Henry Stubbe*, intitled, *A Light fhining out
of Darknefs*, &c. Wherein all the other religious
Parties among us are as handfomly and learnedly
banter'd and ridicul'd, as the *Quakers* have been in
any Book againft them. And when they were attack'd by one *Samuel Young*, a whimfical Prefbyte-
rian-Buffoon-Divine, who call'd himfelf *Trepidan-
tium Malleus*, and fet up for an Imitator of Mr. *Alfop*,
in feveral Pamphlets full of Stories, Repartees, and
Ironies ; in which *Young*, perhaps, thought himfelf
as fecure from a Return of the like kind, as a
Ruffian or Thief may when he affaults Men : His
Attacks were repell'd in a Book intitled " *Trepi-*
" *dantium Malleus intrepidanter malleatus* ; or the
" Weft Country Wifeaker's crack-brain'd *Reprimand*
" hammer'd about his own Numbfcul. Being a *Joco-*
" *fatirical* Return to a late Tale of a Tub, emitted
" by a reverend *Non-con*, at prefent refiding not far
" from *Bedlam*," faid to be written by *William Penn*,
who has therein made ufe of the carnal Weapons
of Irony and Banter, and drefs'd out the Prefbyterian Prieft in a Fool's Coat, for a Spectacle to the
Mob. It is alfo to be obferv'd, that there are feveral
Tracts in the two Volumes of *William Penn's* Works
lately publifh'd, that for ingenious Banter and Irony,
are much fuperior to the Priefts his Adverfaries ; and
that other Quaker Authors profefs to write fometimes in a * *drolling Style.*

XV. The Jacobite Clergy have fet up for great
Droles upon all the true Friends of the *Eftablifhment.*

* *Elwood's Hiftory of his own Life*, &c. *p.* 318.

And

And I prefume, the Body of our High Churchmen would not willingly deprive them of the Benefit of their *Drollery.*

The celebrated Mr. *Collier* * thus attacks Bifhop *Burnet,* for his Essay *on the Memory of Queen* Mary. " This Doctor, you know, is a Man of mighty *La-* " *titude,* and can fay any thing to ferve a Turn ; " whofe *Reverence* refolves Cafes of Confcience " backwards and forwards, difputes *pro* and *con,* " praifes and difpraifes by fecular Meafures ; with " whom Virtue and Vice, paffive Obedience and " Rebellion, Parricide and filial Duty, Treachery " and Faithfulnefs, and all the Contradictions in " Nature, are the *beft* and *worft* things under the " Sun, as they are for his Purpofe, and according " as the Wind fits : who equally and indifferently " writes for and againft all Men, the Gofpel, and him- " felf too, as the World goes : who can beftow a " Panegyrick upon the feven deadly Sins, and (if " there be occafion) can make an Invective againft " all the Commandments.——

In relation to Dr. *Payne*'s *Sermon* on the Death of that *Queen,* he fays †, " that to go thro' it is too " great a Difcipline for any Man, whofe Palate " hath ever relifh'd any thing above *three half-* " *penny Poetry.*' He adds, " Why, Sir, many Years " ago I have heard fome of it fung about the " Streets in wretched and naufeous *Doggrel.* What " think you of this? *Page* 6. *I know not how to* " *draw her Picture, 'tis fo all over beauteous, with-* " *out any Foil, any Shade, any Blemifh ; fo perfect in* " *every Feature, fo accomplifh'd in every Part, fo* " *adorn'd with every Perfection and every Grace.* " O rare, Sir ! here's *Phillis* and *Chloris,* and *Gil-* " *lian a Croydon.*

* *Remarks on fome late Sermons, &c. p.* 34.
‡ *Pag.* 52.

" *Sh'hath*

" *Sh' hath* every Feature, every Grace,
" *So charming* every part, *&c.*

" Tis no wonder he tells us, (*p.* 8.) of *ſtrewing her*
" *with the Flowers of withered and decay'd Poetry* ; for
" the *Song* out of which he hath tranſcrib'd his *Ser-*
" *mon,* is of very *great age,* and hath been ſung
" at many a *Whitſun-Ale,* and many a *Wedding* (tho
" I believe never at a Funeral before) and there-
" fore in all this time may well be *decay'd and*
" *wither'd :* In the mean time, if you were to
" draw the Picture of a *great Princeſs,* I fanſy
" you would not make choice of *Moſſa* to ſit to
" it. Alas! Sir, there was *Caſſandra* and *Cleopa-*
" *tra,* and many a famed *Romance* more, which
" might have furniſh'd him with handſome Cha-
" racters, and yet he muſt needs be *preaching and*
" *inſtructing* his People out of *Hey down derry,* and
" the *fair Maid of* Kent. If he had intitled it,
" *The* White-Chapel *Ballad,* and got ſome body
" to ſet it to the Tune of *Amaryllis,* compos'd by
" *W. P. Songſter,* the Character of the *Author,*
" the *Title,* and the *Matter,* would have very well
" agreed, and perhaps it might have paſſed at the
" Corners of the Streets ; but to call it a *Sermon,*
" and by *W. P.* Doctor in *Divinity,* 'tis one of the
" *lewdeſt* things in the World.———"
Mr. *Leſley* attacks the Clergy, who pray'd " that
" God would give King *James* Victory over all his
" Enemies *, when that was the thing they leaſt
" wiſh'd; and confeſs'd, that they labour'd all they
" could againſt it," ſaying, " good God ! What
" Apprehenſions, what Thought had thoſe Men
" of their publick Prayers ; bantering God Al-

* *Anſwer to* State of the Proteſtants in *Ireland,* &c. *p.* 108.
" mighty,

" mighty, and mocking him to his Face, who heard
" their Words, and faw their Hearts? Is not
" *Atheifm* a fmaller Sin than this, fince it is better
" to have no God, than fo to fet up one *to laugh*
" *at him*."

Again he fays, *(p.* 123.) " It is a fevère Jeft,
" that the common People have got up againft the
" Clergy, that there was but one thing formerly
" which the Parliament could not do, that is, to
" make a Man a Woman : But now there is an-
" other, that is, to make an Oath which the Cler-
" gy will not take."

The fame Author attacks Bifhop *Burnet*'s *Speech
upon the Bill againft Occafional Conformity,* by a Pamphlet intitled, *The Bifhop of* Salisbury*'s proper Defence
from a Speech cry'd about the Streets in his Name, and
faid to have been fpoken by him in the Houfe of Lords upon the Bill againft Occafional Conformity* ; which is one
perpetual *Irony* on the Bifhop, and gives the Author occafion to throw all manner of Satire and
Abufe on the Bifhop. The beginning of this
Pamphlet, which is as follows, will let the Reader
into the full Knowledge of the Defign of the Irony,
and the manner of Execution.

" The Licenfe of this Age and of the Prefs is
" fo great, that no Rank or Quality of Men is
" free from the Infults of loofe and extravagant
" Wits.

" The good Bifhop of *Salisbury* has had a plen-
" tiful Share in this fort of Treatment: And now
" at laft, fome or other has prefum'd to burlefque
" his Lordfhip in printing a Speech for him, which
" none that knows his Lordfhip can believe ever
" came from him.

" But becaufe it may go down with others who
" are too apt to take Slander upon truft, and that
" his Lordfhip has already been pelted with feve-
" ral

" ral Anſwers to his Speech, I have preſum'd to
" offer the following Conſiderations, to clear his
" Lordſhip from the Suſpicion of having vented
" (in ſuch an auguſt Aſſembly) thoſe crude and
" undigeſted Matters which are ſet forth in that
" Speech, and which ſo highly reflect on his Lord-
" ſhip's ſelf."

He has taken the ſame Method of Irony to attack the ſaid Biſhop for his *Speech* on the *Trial* of
Sacheverel, and for a *Sermon*, under this Title, "The
" Good Old Cauſe, *or* Lying in Truth ; being a
" Second Defence of the Lord Biſhop of *Sarum*
" from a Second Speech, and alſo the Diſſection
" of a Sermon it is ſaid his Lordſhip preach'd in
" the Cathedral Church of *Salisbury*." And this
Pamphlet, which is alſo a continued Banter, be-
gins thus.

" No Man has more deſerv'd than this good
" Biſhop, and no Man has been more perſecuted
" by various Ways and Means than his Lordſhip,
" even to mobbing ! But the uglieſt and moſt ma-
" licious of all theſe Arts, is that of putting falſe
" Things upon him ; to write ſcandalous, ſeditious,
" and ſenſeleſs Papers, and to affix his Lordſhip's
" Name ! I was forc'd ſome Years ago to vindi-
" cate his Lordſhip's Reputation from one of this
" ſort : That Speech had a Bookſeller's Name to
" it of good figure, and look'd ſomething like ;
" but this Speech (ſaid likewiſe to be ſpoken in the
" Houſe of Lords) has no body to own it, and has
" all the Marks of *Grub*. But the naſty Phiz is
" nothing to the inſide. That diſcovers the Man ;
" the Heart is falſe."

This ſame Author has thought fit to attack Mr.
Hoadley (ſince a Biſhop) in the way of Banter : His
Beſt

Beſt Anſwer ever was made, and to which no Anſwer will ever be made, is by his own Confeſſion a *Farce* ; when he ſays in his *Preface*, " If you aſk why I treat " this Subject by way of *farce*, and ſhew a little " Merriment ſometimes ? it was becauſe the Foun- " dation you ſtand upon is not only *falſe* but *ridi-* " *culous*, and ought to be treated with the *utmoſt* " *Contempt*."

Again, in his " *Finiſhing Stroke, in defence of* " his *Rehearſals, Beſt Anſwer, and Beſt of all,*" he gives us (*p.* 125.) what he calls, " A Battle-Royal " between three Cocks of the Game, *Higden,* " *Hoadley,* and a *Hottentot*;" which in the *Contents* he calls *A Farce,* and to which he joins both a *Prologue* and *Epilogue,* and divers other Particu- lars, all taken from the *Play-houſe.*

The Reverend Mr. *Matthias Earbery* ſets up for a great Satiriſt and Drole upon the ſwearing and Low- Church Clergy, in numerous Pamphlets of late, more particularly in his " *Serious Admonition to* " *Dr.* Kennet : To which is added, a ſhort but com- " plete Anſwer to Mr. *Marſhal*'s late Treatiſe " called, *A Defence of our Conſtitution in Church* " *and State* ; and a Parallel is drawn between him " and Dr. *Kennet*, for the Satisfaction of the unpre- " judic'd Reader."

He has a bantering Argument * to ſhew, that, " If in future Ages Mr. *Marſhal*'s Book ſhould " eſcape the juſt Judgment it deſerves, of being " condemn'd to the *Paſtry-Cooks* and *Grocers,* an " induſtrious Chronologiſt might make an Ob- " ſervation to prove him too young to write it."

The *Parallel* is in *Pag.* 126. which being very groſs *Raillery,* I only refer you to it.

* *Pag.* 120, 121.

This

This Mr. *Earbery* alſo wrote a *Letter to Biſhop* Fleetwood, under the Title of " A Letter to the " Biſhop of *Ely*, upon the Occaſion of his *ſuppos'd* " late *Charge*, ſaid to be deliver'd at *Cambridge* " *Auguſt* 7, 1716, *&c.*" in which he purſues the Ironical Scheme laid down in the ſaid Title, and endeavours to *vindicate* his *Lordſhip from the Aſper-ſion of writing ſuch a mean Pamphlet*, as the *Charge*.

Nor do theſe *Jacobites* confine their Drollery to their Adverſaries without, but exerciſe it on one a-nother, as may be ſeen in their late Diſpute about King *Edward the Sixth's* Liturgy. And Mr. *Leſley* himſelf, happening to engage on the ſide oppoſite to the Traditions of the Fathers, and attacking thoſe Traditions by Low-Church Notions and Ar-guments, and thereby running counter to all his former Books, is attack'd juſt in the ſame manner he attack'd Biſhop *Burnet*, in a Book under this Title, " Mr. *Leſley's* Defence, from ſome erroneous " and dangerous Principles, advanced in a Letter " ſaid to have been written concerning the New " Separation." And it has ſeveral Paragraphs at the beginning in the very words of one of Mr. *Leſ-ley's* Books againſt the ſaid Biſhop, as may be ſeen on Compariſon.

XVI. *Chriſt-Church* in *Oxford* is no leſs famous for the *Drolling*, than for the *Orthodox* Spirit reign-ing there ; and the former, being judged an excel-lent Method to ſupport the latter, is cultivated a-mong the Youth, and employ'd by the Members of that Society againſt all the ſuppoſed Adverſaries of the Church, and encourag'd by the governing Eccleſiaſticks there and elſewhere.

Among the many, who have receiv'd their Edu-cation there, and been form'd in Drollery, I will only inſtance in the Reverend Dr. *Atterbury* and Dr.

South ; who being as famous for *Drollery* as for *Zeal* for Religion, and applauded for their *Wit* no lefs than for their *Orthodoxy* ; and particularly for imploying the former in behalf of the latter, feem of fufficient Weight to bear down all Attempts to ftifle their Productions. What Confiderations can make us amends for the Lofs of fuch excellent *drolling Writings*, which promote Religion as well as Mirth ?

With what incomparable Mockery, Ridicule and Sarcafm does Dr. *Atterbury* treat all the Low-Church Clergy that come in his way, together with the *Whig* Miniftry and Adminiftration in his feveral *Convocational Tracts* ? Dr. *Wake*, our prefent Arch-bifhop of *Canterbury*, is reprefented by him as wri-ting fo *contumeliously* * of the Clergy, *that had he not inform'd us in his Title Page who he was, we fhould rather have guefs'd him to have been of the Cabal a-gainft Priefts and Prieftcraft, than one of the Order* ; and as wholly govern'd by † *Intereft* in the *Debate*, and as giving us a moft ‡ *fhallow empty Performance* in relation to our Ecclefiaftical Conftitution, which he ‖ *has done his beft to undermine*, as knowing him-felf to be in the wrong ; and as *deferving* any Name or Cenfure, none being *too bad to be beftow'd* on him ; and in fine, as *the leaft of the little officious Pens by which he expects to be traduc'd*.

Dr. *Bentley* is reprefented as *wrote out of Reputation into Preferment* ; which, whether it be a more fe-vere Sarcafm on the Doctor, than on the Govern-ment, is hard to determine ; and befides, it gives Applaufe to one of the moft drolling and bantering Performances that this drolling Age has produc'd, I mean Dr. Bentley's *Differtations on the Epiftles of Phalaris, and the Fables of Æfop, examin'd.*

* *Preface*, p. 14.   † *Pag.* 11. 24.   ‡ *Pag.* 1.
‖ *Pag.* 4, 11, 12, 13, 19.

Bifhop

Bifhop *Burnet* is a ftanding Subject of Ridicule
with him ; as are Bifhop *Nicholfon*, Bifhop *Kennet*,
Bifhop *Gibfon*, Bifhop *Trimnel* [to whom he writes a
moft drolling * Letter] and Dr. *Weft* ; and all the
Topicks that can affect them as Scholars, as ho-
neft Men, and Clergymen, are imploy'd to render
them ridiculons, and fet the World a laughing at
them, who are not in the leaft fpar'd for their being of the Holy Order ; but on the contrary feem
more loaded and baited with Sarcafms for that
reafon.

For a *Specimen*, take this Banter or Burlefque
upon Bifhop *Kennet*'s Dedication of his *Ecclefiaftical
Synods and Parliamentary Convocations*, &c. to the
Archbifhop of *Canterbury* ; which Banter runs thus †.

" *May it pleafe your Grace*,
" Mr. *Atterbury* has lately forc'd a Dedication
" upon you, which favours too much of Prefump-
" tion or Defign ; he has prefum'd to furprize you
" with an unexpected Addrefs, and appears very
" indecently before your Grace, becaufe he has
" taken no care to exprefs upon this Subject a due
" Refpect and Reverence to the Governors in
" Church and State, fuch as is fuitable to the Chri-
" ftian Religion, and his particular Function: The
" Reports and Authorities in his Book are Fruits of
" other Mens Collections, not the immediate Ef-
" fects of his own Searches into *Regifters* and *Re-
" cords* ; he imperioufly fummons your Grace and
" my Lords the Bifhops to an immediate Compli-
" ance upon pain of being pronounc'd Betrayers of
" the Church ——This, my Lord, is the Character
" of the Perfon *I fet up* againft ; but as for me, I

---

* Appendix to Parliamentary Original, &c. *p.* 14.
† Some Remarks on the Temper of fome late Writers, &c.
p. 33.

" am

" am quite another fort of Man, I am very well
" bred, a great Antiquary, beholden to no body,
" *fome Wits and merry Folks call me a Tool and a*
" *Play-thing (Pref. p.* 8.) But I affure your Grace,
" that what Freedom foever I may have taken in
" taxing the Vices of the inferior Clergy, (*p.* 77.
" 188.) and in reflecting *upon the ambitious Defigns*
" *of dignify'd Presbyters* (*p.* 196.) ; yet *I am however*
" *tender and dutiful in treating the Governors of our*
" *Church* (p. 78.) ; efpecially *thofe of them who are*
" *of the Ecclefiaftical Commiffion for Preferments,*
" (p. 311). I have a very great Refpect and Re-
" verence for every body that will give me any
" thing ; and how refolute foever Mr. *Atterbury*
" may be, your Grace may do what you pleafe with

Your Grace's moft humble

and obedient Servant,

WHITE KENNET.

But for *Drollery,* the Reverend Dr. *South* outdoes
even *Chrift-Church,* and fills all his Performances
with it, and throws it out againft the Enemies of the
Church, and in particular againft the late Dr. *Sherlock,* whom he thought fit to fingle out. I fhall
felect fome Paffages from his Writings againft the
faid Doctor, which cannot but entertain the High-
Church Orthodox Reader, and reconcile him to a
Drollery fo well employ'd.

He ftiles him *a great good Man, as a certain poor
Wretch,* meaning *Prior, calls him.*

Again, he fays *, " There is hardly any one Sub-
" ject which he (that is Dr. *Sherlock) has wrote up-

* **Preface to Animad.** *p.* 12, 13.

"on,

' on Popery excepted', that he has wrote both for
" it and againft it. Could any thing be more fharp
" and bitter againft the Diffenters than what this
" Man wrote in his *Anfwer* to the *Proteftant Re-*
" *conciler*; and yet how frankly, or rather fulfomly
" does he open both his Arms to embrace them in
" his Sermon preach'd before the Lord Mayor on
" *November* 4, 1688. Tho I dare fay, that the
" Diffenters themfelves are of that Conftancy, as
" to own that they were of the fame Principles in
" 88 that they were of in 85 ; but the Truth is, old
" Friendfhips cannot be fo eafily forgot: And it has
" been an Obfervation made by fome, that hardly
" can any one be found, who was firft tainted with
" a Conventicle, whom a Cathedral could ever after
" cure, but that ftill upon every crofs turn of Af-
" fairs againft the *Church*, the irrefiftible *Magne-*
" *tifm* of the *Good Old Caufe* (as fome ftill think it)
" would quickly draw him out of the *Good Old Way*.
" The Fable tells us of a *Cat* once turn'd into a
" *Woman*, but the next fight of a *Moufe* quickly
" diffolv'd the *Metamorphofis*, cafhier'd the Wo-
" man, and reftor'd the Brute. And fome *Virtuofi*
" (fkill'd in the *ufeful Philofophy* of *Alterations*)
" have thought her much a Gainer by the latter
" Change, there being fo many unlucky Turns in
" the World, in which it is not half fo fafe and
" advantageous to *walk upright*, as to be *able to fall*
" *always upon one's Legs*."
  Again, Dr. *South* fays *, " When I confider how
" wonderfully pleas'd the Man is with thefe two
" new ftarted Terms (*Self-confcioufnefs* and *mutual*
" *Confcioufnefs*) fo high in Sound and fo empty of
" Senfe, inftead of one fubftantial word (*Omni-*

---

* Animad. *p.* 114.

E   *fcience*)

" *science)* which gives us all that can be pretended
" useful in them, with vast Overplus and Advan-
" tage, and even swallows them up, as *Moses's* Rod
" did those pitiful Tools of the *Magicians:* This
" *(* I say) brings to my mind (whether I will or no)
" a certain Story of a grave Person, who riding
" in the Road with his Servant, and finding himself
" something uneasy in his Saddle, bespoke his Ser
" vant thus: *John* (says he) *alight, and first take off*
" *the Saddle that is upon my Horse, and then take off*
" *the Saddle that is upon your Horse ; and when you*
" *have done this, put the Saddle that was upon my*
" *Horse, upon your Horse ; and put the Saddle that*
" *was upon your Horse, upon my Horse.* Whereup-
" on the Man, who had not studied the Philoso-
" phy of Saddles (whether *Ambling* or *Trotting*) so
" exactly as his Master, replies something short upon
" him ; *Lord, Master, what need all these words?*
" *Could you not as well have said, Let us change Sad-*
" *dles?* Now I must confess, I think the Servant
" was much in the right ; tho the Master having a
" *rational Head of his own,* and being withal wil-
" ling to make the *Notion* of *changing* Saddles more
" *plain, easy* and *intelligible,* and to give a clearer
" Explication of that word (which his Forefathers,
" how good *Horsemen* soever they might have
" been, yet were *not equally happy in explaining of*)
" was pleas'd to set it forth by that more full and
" accurate Circumlocution."

He says *, *The Author*, Dr. *Sherlock, is no doubt a*
Grecian *in his Heart!* And the tenth Chapter of the
Animadversions is one continued Banter upon the
Dean for his Ignorance in *Greek* and *Latin,* and
even his Inability to spell: All which he *closes*

* Ibid. *p.* 332.

with

with faying, " That St. *Paul*'s School is certainly
" an excellent School, and St. *Paul*'s Church a moft
" noble Church ; and therefore he thinks that he
" directs his Courfe very prudently, and happily
" too, who in his Paffage to fuch a *Cathedral*,
" takes a School in his way."

Again, he fays *, " He cannot fee any new Ad-
" vantage that the Dean has got over the *Soci-*
" *nians*, unlefs it be, that the Dean thinks his
" *three Gods* will be too hard for their *one*."

After citing feveral Scurrilities of the Dean †, (who
it muft be confefs'd, appears therein a great Banterer alfo of Dr. *South* and his Performance) the
Dr. fays, " Thefe, with feveral more of the like
" *Gravel-Lane* Elegancies, are all of them fuch
" peculiar Strictures of the Dean's *Genius*, that
" he might very well fpare his Name, where he
" had made himfelf fo well known by his Mark ;
" for all the foregoing *Oyfter-Wive-Kennel-Rhetorick*
" feems fo naturally to flow from him, who had
" been fo long Rector of St. *Botolph* (with the well-
" fpoken *Billingfgate* under his Care) that (as much a
" Teacher as he was) it may well be queftion'd,
" whether he has learn'd more from his Parifh, than
" his Parifh from him.---All favours of the Porter,
" the Carman, and the Waterman ; and a pleafant
" Scene it muft be to fee the *Mafter of the Tem-*
" *ple* laying about him in the Language of the
" Stairs."

To the Dean's Scoff, that *this Argument*, &c. *was
worth its weight in Gold, tho the Dean fears it will
not much enrich the Buyer*, the Doctor replies ‡, " What
" is that to him ? Let him mind his own Markets,
" who never writes to *enrich the Buyer* but the Sel-

---

* Ibid. *p.* 348.
† Tritheifm charged, *p.* 2, 3.   ‡ Ib. *p.* 108.

E 2   " ler ;

" ler; and that *Seller* is himself : and since he is
" so, well is it for his Books and his Booksel-
" ler too, that Men generally *buy* before they.
" *read*.

In requital of the scurrilous Character of an
ingenious Blunderer, Dr. *South* says *, " He must here
" return upon him the just Charge of an *impious*
" *Blasphemer*, and that upon more Accounts than
" one ; telling him withal, that had he liv'd in the
" former Times of the Church, his Gown would
" have been stript off his Back for his detestable
" Blasphemies and Heresies, and some other Place
" found out for him to perch in than the Top of
" St. *Paul's*, where at present he is placed like a true
" Church Weather-Cock, (as he is) notable for
" nothing so much, as *standing high and turning*
" *round*."

Again, he says †, " And so I take my leave of the
" Dean's *three distinct infinite Minds, Spirits,* or *Sub-*
" *stances,* that is to say, of his *three Gods ;* and having
" done this, methinks I see him go whimpering
" away with his Finger in his Eye, and the Com-
" plaint of *Micah* in his Mouth, *Ye have taken away*
" *my Gods which I made, and what have I more ‡?*
" Tho he must confess, he cannot tell why he
" should be so fond of them, since he dares under-
" take that he will never be able to bring the
" Christian World either to believe in, or to wor-
" ship a *Trinity of Gods :* Nor does he see what
" use they are likely to be of, even to himself, un-
" less peradventure to *swear by.*

Again, the Doctor says §, " The Dean's follow-
" ing Instruction to his Friend is certainly very di-
" verting, in these words, where the Animadverter

* Ibid. *p.* 170. † Ibid. *p.* 281. ‡ Judg. 18. 24.
§ Ib. *p.* 285

" charges

" charges the Dean with Abſurdities and Contra-
" dictions ; turn to the Place and read it with its
" Context, and tell me what you cannot anſwer,
" and I will; to which he would have done well to
" have added, *If I can.* But the whole Paſſage is
" juſt as if he had ſaid, Sir, if you find not Con-
" tradictions and Abſurdities enough in my Book to
" ſatisfy your Curioſity that way, pray come to
" the Fountain-head, and conſult me, and you
" ſhall be ſure of a more plentiful Supply."

Again, upon the Dean's " Frequent reproach-
" ing the * Animadverter with the Character of a
" *Wit*, tho join'd with ſuch ill-favour'd Epithets,
" as his witleſs Malice has thought fit to degrade it
" with, as that he is *a ſpiteful Wit*, a *wrangling*
" *Wit*, a *ſatirical Wit*, and the W i t t y, *ſubtle*,
" *good-natur'd Animadverter, &c.* the Dr. ſays,
" that tho there be but little *Wit* ſhewn in ma-
" king ſuch Charges ; yet if *Wit* be a *Reproach* (be
" it of what ſort it will) the Animadverter is too *juſt*
" to return this *Reproach* upon the *Defender* ; and
" withal, underſtands himſelf, and what becomes
" him, too well, either to *aſſume* to himſelf, or
" ſo much as to *admit* the Character of a *Wit*, as
" at all due to him ; eſpecially ſince he knows that
" *common Senſe* (a thing much ſhort of Wit) is enough
" to enable him to deal with ſuch an Adverſary.
" Nevertheleſs, there are many in the World, who
" are both call'd and accounted *Wits*, and really
" are ſo ; which (one would think) ſhould derive
" ſomething of Credit upon this Qualification,
" even in the Eſteem of this Author himſelf, or at
" leaſt rebate the Edge of his Invectives againſt it,
" conſidering that it might have pleas'd God to
" have made him a *Wit* too."

* Ibid. *p.* 199.

E 3   XVII. As

XVII. As things now ftand, it may eafily be feen, that Profecutions for *Raillery* and *Irony* would not be relifh'd well by the Publick, and would probably turn to the Difreputation and Difgrace of the Profecutor.

Archbifhop *Laud* has always been much cenfur'd for his malicious Profecution of *Williams* in the *Star-Chamber*; among whofe Crimes I find the following laid to his Charge : * *That he faid all Flefh in* England *had corrupted their Ways* ; that *he call'd a Book intitled,* A Coal from the Altar (written by Dr. *Heylin,* for placing the Communion-Table at the Eaft-end of the Church, and railing it in) *a Pamphlet* ; that *he fcoffingly faid, that he had heard of a Mother Church, but not of a Mother Chapel,* meaning the King's, to which all Churches in Ceremony *ought to conform* ; that *he wickedly jefted on St.* Martin'*s Hood* ; that *he faid the People ought not to be lafh'd by every body's Whip* ; that *he faid,* (citing *a National Council for it) that the People are* God'*s and the King's, and not the Prieft's People* ; and *that he doth not allow Priefts to jeer and make Invectives againft the People.* And I humbly conceive, that fuch Matters had much better be fuffer'd to go on in the World, and take their Courfe, than that Courts of Judicature fhould be employ'd about them. A Sentence that imply'd fome *Clergymen* corrupt, as well as fome *Laymen,* of whom *Laud* would only allow to have it faid, that they had *corrupted their Ways* ; a *Jeft* upon St. *Martin's Hood,* which, according to Ecclefiaftical Hiftory, *cur'd fore Eyes* ; and a *Ridicule* upon a High-Church Book of *Heylin's,* by calling it a Pamphlet, tho it was really a Pamphlet, as confifting of but feventy

* *Fuller's* Church Hiftory, Cent. 17. B. 11. Sect. 89. Parag. 10.

Pages

Pages in Quarto; feem lefs *wicked* and hurtful than difturbing, fining, and undoing Men about them. And the having fome Concern for the People, that they fhould not be ufed as the Prieft pleas'd ; that the *People* belong to *God* and the *King*, and *not to the Prieft* ; and the *not allowing* the *Priefts* to *jeer and make Invectives againft the People* ; feem all Errors fit to be born with.

Archbifhop *Laud* was alfo thought guilty of an exceffive Piece of Weaknefs in the Punifhment of * *Archibald* the King's Fool, by laying the Matter before the Privy-Council, and occafioning him to be expell'd the King's Houfe for a poor *Jeft* upon himfelf ; who, as he was a Man at the Head of the State, fhould have defpis'd fuch a thing in any Body, much more in a *Fool*, and who fhould never have been hurried on to be the Inftrument of any *Motion* againft him, but have left it to others ; who upon the leaft Intimation would have been glad to make their court to *Laud*, by facrificing a *Fool* only to his Refentment.

XVIII. I could have entertain'd the Reader with a great Variety of Paffages out of the Fathers of the Church, whofe Writings are Magazines of Authority, and urg'd upon us upon all Occafions by Ecclefiafticks, and are particularly full of *Burlefque* and *Ridicule* on the *Gods and Religion* of the *Pagans*; in the ufe whereof they are much more unanimous, than in the Articles of their *Creed*. But that being a Subject too great and extenfive for a Digreffion, I fhall content my felf with the few followingReflections ; which will fufficiently evince, that the *Tafte* of the Primitive Chriftians was like that of the reft

* *Rufhworth*, Part II. Vol. I. *p.* 471.

of

of the World ; that they could laugh and be as merry as the *Greeks* and other *Pagans* ; and that they would take the Advantage of the *Pagans* weak Caufe, to introduce *Ridicule*, which always bears hard upon Weaknefs and Folly, and muft load them fo as to prevent a Poffibility of their being remov'd by another *Ridicule*.

These Fathers have transfufed into their Writings all the Wit and Raillery of the antient *Pagan* Writers and Philofophers ; who it is well known wrote a great deal to turn *Paganifm* into Ridicule ; moft of which now exifts no where but in the Works of the Fathers ; all Books of that kind being loft, except *Cicero*'s Books of *the Nature of Gods*, and of *Divination*, and the Dialogues of *Lucian* ; both which Authors have been of great ufe to the *Fathers* to fet them up for *Wits*, *Droles*, and *Satirifts*. For a Specimen how well thefe antient *Pagans* could *drole*, and how much beholden we are to the Fathers for recording their Drolleries, the moft remarkable, I think, are fome *Fragments* of a Book of *Oenomaus* concerning the *Pagan Oracles*, cited and preferv'd by * *Eufebius* ; who has given us occafion to † *regret* the lofs of this Work, as one of the moft valuable Books written by the Antients on the Subject of *Oracles*, tho thofe Books were *very numerous*. And it is to be obferv'd, that this Book and a great many, perhaps a ‖ thoufand more, were publifh'd in *Greece*, where the Impofture of *Oracles* greatly prevail'd, and great Wealth flow'd in, not only to the Priefts of the *Oracular Temples*, but to all the Inhabitants of *Greece*, and efpecially to thofe who lived in the Neighbourhood of the feveral

* *Præp. Evang.* l. 4. p. 209-234.
† Fontenelle, Hiftorie des Oracles. 1. Differt. c. vii.
‖ Eufeb. Id. l. 4.

Ora-

Oracular Temples ; who made a great Profit from the rich Travellers, that came from all Parts of the World to know their Fortunes. This ſhews the great Integrity and Fairneſs of the old *Pagans* ; who would ſuffer not only their ſuppoſed ſtanding Revelation to be call'd in quſtion, but a Revelation that brought in as much Money, as the Chapels, Churches, and Shrines dedicated to the Bleſſed Virgin, or to any of the Saints, do in the *Roman* Church, without calling any Man to Account for the Liberties they took ; who, as far as appears, were not expos'd ** *to any Danger* thereby. It is alſo to be obſerv'd, that the merry †† *Epicureans were none of them ever proſecuted*, and *that* Epicurus himſelf *died quietly at* Athens *in a very great old Age*.

But the Book, which the Fathers made the moſt uſe of, was that arch, ſly, and drolling Performance, now loſt, of *Evemerus*, which he intitled, *A ſacred Hiſtory :* wherein he gave an *hiſtorical Account* of the *Birth, Country, Lives, Deaths*, and *Burials* of the *Gods*. This Work was tranſlated into *Latin* by that arch Wag *Ennius*, who himſelf has moſt ingeniouſly *ridicul'd* ſeveral Impoſtors or very grave Perſons, in a remarkable Piece of Poetry, which I ſhall give my Reader in *Engliſh*.

" *I value not a Ruſh the* Marſian *Augur,*
" *Nor Country-Fortune Tellers, nor Town-Star-Gazers,*
" *Nor jugling Gypſies, nor yet Dream-Interpreters :*
" *For, not by Skill or Art, are theſe Diviners ;*
" *But ſuperſtitious Prophets, Gueſſers impudent,*
" *Or idle Rogues, or craz'd, or mere ſtarving Beggars.*
" *They know no way themſelves, yet others would direct ;*
" *And crave a Groat of thoſe, to whom they promiſe Riches :*
" *Thence let them take the Groat, and give back all the reſt.*

** **Baltus,** Suite de la Reponſe a l'Hiſ. des Oracles, *p.* 283.
†† *Ibid.*

XIX. Wherefore I cannot but prefume, that an Attempt to make a *Law* to reftrain *Irony*, &c. would prove abortive, and that the Attempt would be deem'd the Effeft of a very partial Confideration of things, and of prefent Anger at a poor Jeft; which Men are not able to bear themfelves, how much foever they abound in *Jefts*, both of the *light* and *cruel* kind, on others: tho for my own part I concur heartily with you in *making* fuch a *Law*, and in leaving it to a Perfon of your *Equity* to draw it up, craving only the Liberty to propofe an Amendment or Addition, *viz.* that you would be pleas'd to infert a Claufe to prevent *Irony, Ridicule*, and *Banter*, from invading the Pulpit, and particularly to prevent pointing out *Perfons of Men* * from thence, and reviling them, as alfo reviling whole Bodies of Men: For whatever is immoral in Print, is, in my Opinion, immoral in the Pulpit. Befides, thefe things feem more improper in the Pulpit, than they can be in Print: becaufe no *Reprifals* can be made in the former, as in the latter Cafe; where they, or the Fear of them, may give fome Check to the Diforder, and reduce things to a tolerable Temper and Decency. If, in order to juftify my Motion, it could be thought neceffary or proper here to give a Detail of ridiculing and ironical Paffages, taken from Sermons againft particular Men, and Bodies of Men, and their Doctrines, you cannot but know how eafy it would be to fill a Volume with them, without going to Authors, who have occafionally produc'd abundance of them. And I will only mention here a Paffage in a *Volume of Sermons*, juft now publifh'd, of a well known *High Divine*, the Reverend Mr. *Wil-*

---

* *Bp. Hoadley. Anfwer to the Reprefentation, &c. Pref. p. 12.*

William Reeves, made famous by his *Tranſlation* of ſome *Apologies of the Primitive Fathers*, which gain'd him the Applauſes of a great many *High Men*, and particularly *Hickes*, *Dodwel*, and *Nelſon*, &c. and a Recommendation from the laſt to the Queen, who in the latter end of her Reign made him *Chaplain in Ordinary*, and obtain'd for him a conſiderable Preferment. This Gentleman, attacking Biſhop *Hoadley*'s *Sermon* of *The Kingdom of Chriſt*, ſays *, " In theſe laſt Days we have been
" taught to be as indolent and unconcern'd as
" poſſible in the Service of God : A noted *Novelliſt*
" [Bp. *Hoadley*] among many other odd *Engines*,
" hath invented one, to pump out all Devotion
" from Prayer, and make it a *Vacuum*. Inſtead of
" the old fervent, affectionate way of Worſhip-
" ping, he hath ſubſtituted a new Idol, a Vanity, a
" Nothing of his own, *a calm and undiſturb'd Ad-*
" *dreſs to God.*—— The *Arrows* and *bitter Words*
" Mr. *Hales* hath levell'd againſt *Rome* only, our
" Right Reverend hath *pointed a-new*, and ſhot
" them full againſt the Church he ſuperintends,
" and with all the Force of inbred, fanatick Fury.
" And by this time ſurely it is well known, that
" he is a very *warm Man* in every thing, but his
" *Prayers.*"

XX. Inſtead of addreſſing the foregoing Papers to you, I could have addreſs'd them to ſeveral others ; who of late have thought fit to recognize the Right of Men, to examine into, and judge for themſelves in all Matters of ſpeculation, and eſpecially in Matters of mere Religion, and to publiſh their Reaſons againſt any Opinions they judge erroneous, tho publickly receiv'd in the Country where they live, provided they do it *ſeri-*

---

* *Page* 91.

ouſly

ously and *gravely:* which is a noble Progrefs in Truth, and owing to that glorious Liberty, and Freedom of Debate, that we enjoy under our moft excellent Princes ; and which extorts it even from them, who, to have fome Credit in the World, are forced to own, what would difcredit them to go on to deny, among all who have any degree of *Virtue, Senfe,* and *Learning.* But I was determin'd to addrefs my felf to you, as a Perfon of more remarkable *Moderation* than ordinary in your *Letter* to Dr. *Rogers:* And one, who had, long before, in your *Defence of the Conftitution in Church and State* ; in anfwer to the *Charge of the Nonjurors,* accufing us of *Herefy and Schifm,* Perjury *and* Treafon, " valu'd || and commended the In-" tegrity of the Nonjurors in declaring their Senti-" ments:" and who, tho you juftly charge thofe of them you write againft, " as attacking us with fuch " uncommon Marks of Violence * as moft plainly " intimate, that no Meafures are intended to be " kept with us by them in the Day of their Prof-" perity, who in the Day of their Adverfity, even " when they are moft at Mercy, cannot refrain " from fuch *raging* Provocations ; but when re-" duced to the Neceffity of *taking* Quarter, profefs " moft plainly they will never give it :" Yet as to thefe Enemies, who would deftroy our Church and State, and † " revive upon us the Charge of *Here-* " *fy* and *Schifm,* Perjury *and* Treafon, Crimes of " no fmall figure either in the Law or in the Gof-" pel," you only fay, that " if you may have " leave to borrow a Thought from ‡ one of their " own moft celebrated Writers, you would tell " them, that *the Blood and Spirits were made to rife* " *upon fuch Occafions :* Nature defign'd not, that

|| *Page* 2.
* *Page* 1.　† *Page* 4, 5.　‡ *Mr.* Collier.

" we

" we fhould be cold or indifferent in our manner
" of receiving, or returning, fuch foul Reproaches."
This is great Moderation, and fuch as I heartily
approve, being difpos'd to forgive the Punifhment
due by Law to any Fault, when the Non-execu-
tion of it will not overturn the Government. And
I am willing to hope, that fince you can think
that fuch bitter Adverfaries to you, as thefe licentious *Jacobites* are, fhould only be fmartly replied to, and not be profecuted by the Government, you will, upon Reflection, think, that a
merry, good humour'd Adverfary fhould be treated
as well.

Tho I have endeavour'd to defend the Ufe of
Ridicule and *Irony*, yet it is fuch *Irony* and *Ridicule*
only as is fit for polite Perfons to ufe. As to the
grofs *Irony* and *Ridicule*, I difapprove of it, as I do
other Faults in Writing ; only I would not have
Men punifh'd, or any other way difturb'd about it,
than by a Return of *Ridicule* and *Irony*. This I
think fit to conclude with, more to prevent Mif-
reprefentation from others, than from you ; whom
I look on to have too much Senfe and Integrity to
miftake or mifreprefent me.

I am Yours, &c.

F I N I S.